SHADOW SQUADRON

PHANTOM SUN

WRITTEN BY
CARL BOWEN

ILLUSTRATED BY
WILSON TORTOSA
AND
BENNY FUENTES

2012.241

AUTHORIZING

SCHOLASTIC INC.

5514.108

ISBN 978-0-545-78046-9

Published by Scholastic Inc., 557 Broadway, New York, NY 10012, by arrangement with Stone Arch Books, a Capstone Imprint.

12 11 10 9 8 7 6 5 4 3 2 14 15 16 17 18 19/0

Printed in the U.S.A. 40

First Scholastic printing, September 2014

Design by Brann Garvey

CONTENTS

1316.981

2012.101

ACCESS GRANTED

CLASSIFIED

SHADOW SQUADRON DOSSIER

CROSS, RYAN

RANK: Lieutenant Commander
BRANCH: Navy Seal
PSYCH PROFILE: Cross is the team leader of Shadow Squadron. Control oriented and loyal, Cross insisted on hand-picking each member of his squad.

WALKER, ALONSO

RANK: Chief Petty Officer
BRANCH: Navy Seal
PSYCH PROFILE: Walker is Shadow Squadron's second-in-command. His combat experience, skepticism, and distrustful nature make him a good counter-balance to Cross's leadership.

YAMASHITA, KIMIYO

RANK: Lieutenant
BRANCH: Army Ranger
PSYCH PROFILE: The team's sniper is an expert marksman and a true stoic. It seems his emotions are as steady as his trigger finger.

BRIGHTON, EDGAR

RANK: Staff Sergeant
BRANCH: Air Force Combat Controller
PSYCH PROFILE: The team's technician and close-quarters-combat specialist is popular with his squadmates but often agitates his commanding officers.

PHOTO NOT AVAILABLE

JANNATI, ARAM

RANK: Second Lieutenant
BRANCH: Army Ranger
PSYCH PROFILE: Jannati serves as the team's linguist. His sharp eyes serve him well as a spotter, and he's usually paired with Yamashita on overwatch.

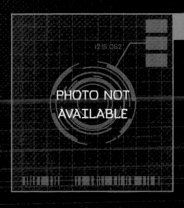

PHOTO NOT AVAILABLE

SHEPHERD, MARK

RANK: Lieutenant
BRANCH: Army (Green Beret)
PSYCH PROFILE: The heavy-weapons expert of the group, Shepherd's love of combat borders on unhealthy.

CLASSIFIED

OPERATION

PHANTOM SUN

5678

An unknown aircraft has crashed in Antarctica near a remote science facility. Shadow Squadron has been tasked with recovering the device. Early reports show that Russian Special Forces are already on the scene, meaning we need to keep a low profile and avoid hostilities if at all possible.

Upon landing, we'll rendezvous with a psy-ops spook from Phantom Cell who has more information on the situation. I don't need to remind you, gentlemen, that stealth is of paramount importance for this mission.

3245.88

– Lieutenant Commander Ryan Cross

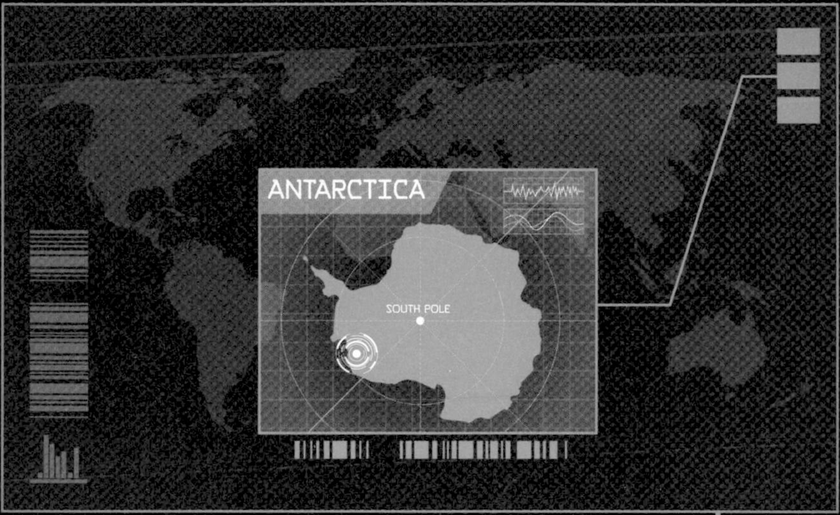

PRIMARY OBJECTIVE(S)

- Locate & secure crashed aircraft
- Maintain anonymity

SECONDARY OBJECTIVE(S)

- Avoid hostilities with Russian Special Forces

INTEL

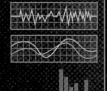

DECRYPTING

12345

COM CHATTER

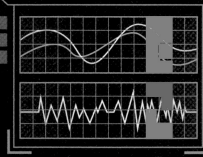

- INTEL: intelligence, or information relevant to a mission
- JSOC: Joint Special Operations Command, or Command for short
- PSY-OPS: psychological operations
- PT: physical training
- SONIC BOOM: a loud noise made when passing the speed of sound

3245.98

CHAPTER ONE

1324.014

SONIC BOOM

Lieutenant Commander Ryan Cross was already in the briefing room when the rest of his team arrived. Shadow Squadron had been carefully pieced together from only the most elite soldiers of the special operations forces of the various US military branches. Represented among them were Navy SEALs, Green Berets, Army Rangers, an Air Force Combat Controller, a Navy corpsman, and a Marine Force Recon specialist.

In short, Shadow Squadron was the top special operations team, and the average citizen knew absolutely nothing about them. Shadow Squadron was tasked with secretly protecting America's interests and defending its people through top-secret, black operations all over the world. They took action where the regular forces would not or could not go.

Lieutenant Commander Cross was proud and honored to serve as the squad's commanding officer. At the moment, however, the seven men under his direct command didn't give the impression that they shared his honor and pride in their work. In fact, they didn't look much like the squad of highly trained professionals that he knew they were. Right now, more than anything, they looked tired. It was just after 0500 hours local time, and none of them shared his enthusiasm for the dawn's early light.

The men filed in quietly with heavy eyes and slow footsteps, many of them clutching mugs of steaming coffee. Each of them carried English muffin sandwiches stuffed full of scrambled eggs, bacon, ham, cheese, and whatever else they could shovel in.

"All right, you herd of turtles," the last man

grumbled as he came into the room. "Shuffle in and sit down."

The speaker was Chief Petty Officer Alonso Walker, Cross's second-in-command. Like Cross, Walker had come to Shadow Squadron from the Navy SEALs, though his training had been more focused and specialized than Cross's. Walker had been with the team since the creation of the program. In the beginning, Walker had resented Cross's authority. Recently, however, Walker had grown to like Cross — and showed him respect on and off the battlefield.

Walker demonstrated that respect by coming into the briefing room balancing an extra breakfast sandwich on top of his own and precariously clinging to the handle of a second mug of coffee in his other hand. The Chief set the extra sandwich and coffee down in front of Cross, then took his position at the other corner.

"Thanks, Chief," Cross said. "You didn't have to do that." Cross neglected to add the reason why: he'd already eaten breakfast an hour ago.

"No problem," Walker grumbled, barely audible, as he hunched over his coffee, avoiding eye contact with everyone. "So is there a reason we're having this briefing before we've even done PT?"

"Yep," Cross replied. He took a sip of coffee for the sake of politeness — it was pitch black, the way Walker liked it.

Cross tapped the touchscreen on the surface of the table. A section of the wall slid open to reveal a high-definition LED screen. It showed the swords-and-globe emblem of the Joint Special Operations Command. Another tap and swipe brought up a still image of two men wearing heavy, red snow parkas as they rode away on a snowmobile. The camera peered over the shoulder of another parka-clad individual on a second snowmobile. Both vehicles made their way across a desolate, white expanse of snow and ice under a gray sky.

At the sight of the image, Staff Sergeant Edgar Brighton gasped in excitement and immediately sucked a mouthful of his breakfast down the wrong pipe. He pointed at the screen, his eyes watering, as he coughed and choked.

"Medic," Cross said dryly.

"I just saw this!" Brighton finally managed to say. "It's real? Are we dealing with this?"

"Why is Brighton freaking out?" Walker asked.

"It's real," Cross replied to Brighton first. He addressed his next word to Walker and the others. "Watch."

At that, Cross tapped his touchscreen to start the video. The thrum of the snowmobiles' engines and the whistling of hard wind burst from the speakers in the briefing room. Cross tapped the touchscreen once more to mute the video.

"You're not missing anything without sound," he explained as the men in red rode through the snow. The camera bobbed and bounced with the motion of the snowmobile in the hands of the person carrying it. "These guys are geologists from Lost Aspen, an American mobile research station in Marie Byrd Land, in western Antarctica. What they're up to here isn't relevant to our mission." He checked the screen and waited for a visual cue, then said, "But this is."

“And it’s flippin’ awesome!” Brighton added.

On the screen, the geologists started pointing and waving frantically. The lead snowmobile’s passenger shook the shoulders of the driver, who then brought the snowmobile to a halt. The cameraman’s driver stopped alongside them. More frantic gesturing from the first geologist made the rest look up to see what he was pointing at. The camera watched them for a few more seconds, then lurched around in a half circle and tilted skyward. Clouds wavered in and out of focus for a second before the cameraman found what the others had pointed at — a lance of white fire in the sky. The image focused, showing what appeared to be a meteorite, with a trailing white plume, punching through a hole in the clouds. The camera zoomed out to allow the cameraman to better track the meteorite’s progress through the sky.

“Is that a meteorite?” Shepherd asked.

“Just keep watching,” Brighton said, breathless with anticipation.

Right on cue, the supposed meteorite suddenly

ared white, then changed directions in mid-flight by almost 45 degrees. Grunts and hisses of surprise filled the room.

"So… not a meteorite," Shepherd muttered.

The members of Shadow Squadron watched in awe as the falling object changed direction once again, with another flare, and pitched downward. The camera angle twisted overhead and then lowered to track its earthward trajectory.

"And now… sonic boom," Brighton said.

The camera image shook violently as the compression wave from the falling object broke the speed of sound and the accompanying burst shook the cameraman's hands. A moment later, the object streaked into the distance and disappeared into the rolling hills of ice and snow. The video footage ended a few moments later with a still image of the gawking geologists looking like a bunch of kids on Christmas morning.

"This video popped up on the Internet a few hours ago," Cross said. "It's already starting to go viral."

"What is it?" Second Lieutenant Aram Jannati said. Jannati, the team's newest member, came from the Marine Special Operations Regiment. "I can't imagine we'd get involved in this if it was just a meteor."

"Meteorite," Staff Sergeant Adam Paxton said. "If it gets through the atmosphere to the ground, it's a meteorite, not a meteor."

Brighton hopped out of his chair. "That wasn't a meteorite, man," he said. He dug his smartphone out of a pocket and came around the table toward the front of the room. He laid his phone on the touchscreen Cross had, then synced up the two devices. With that done, Brighton used his phone as a remote control to run the video backward to the first time the object had changed directions. He used a slider to move the timer back and forth, repeatedly showing the object's sharp angle of deflection through the sky.

"Meteorites can't change directions like this," Brighton said. "This is 45 degrees of deflection at least, and the thing barely even slows down. And it did it *twice*."

"I'm seeing a flare when it turns," Paxton said. "Meteors hold a lot of frozen water when they're in space, and it expands when it reaches the atmosphere. If those gases vented or exploded, couldn't that cause a change in direction?"

"Not this sharply," Brighton said before Cross could reply. "Besides, if you look at this..." He used a few swipes across his phone to pause the video and zoom in on the flying object. At the new resolution, a dark oblong shape was visible inside a wreath of fire. He then advanced through the first and second changes of direction and tracked it a few seconds forward before pausing again. "See?"

A room full of shrugs and uncomprehending looks met Brighton's eager gaze.

Brighton tossed his hands up in mock frustration. "It's the same size!" he said. "If this thing had exploded twice — with enough force to push something this big in a different direction both times — it would be in a million pieces. So those aren't explosions. They're thrusters or ramjets or something."

"Which makes this what?" Shepherd asked. "A UFO?"

"Sure," Paxton answered in a mocking tone. "It's unidentified, it's flying, and it's surely an object."

"You don't know that it's not a UFO," Brighton said. "I mean, this thing could very well be from outer space!"

"Sit down, Sergeant," Chief Walker said.

Brighton reluctantly did so and pocketed his phone.

"Don't get ahead of yourself, Ed," Cross added, retaking control of the briefing. "Phantom Cell analysts have authenticated the video and concluded that this thing is some kind of metal construct, though they can't make out specifics from the quality of the video. I suppose it's possible it's from outer space, but it's much more likely it's man-made. The only thing we know for sure is that it's not American-made. Therefore, our mission is to get out to where it came down, zip it up, and bring it back for a full analysis. Any questions so far?"

“I have one,” Jannati said. “What is Phantom Cell?”

Cross nodded. As the newest member of the team, Jannati wasn’t as familiar with the JSOC’s various secret programs. “Phantom Cell is a parallel program to ours,” Cross explained. “But their focus is on psy-ops, cyberwarfare, and research and development.”

Jannati nodded. “Geeks, in other words,” he said. Brighton gave him a sour look but said nothing.

“What are we supposed to do about the scientists who found this thing?” Lieutenant Kimiyo Yamashita asked. True to his stoic and patient nature, the sniper had finished his breakfast and coffee while everyone else was talking excitedly. “Do they know we’re coming?”

Cross frowned. “That’s the problem,” he said. “We haven’t heard a peep out of them since this video appeared online. Attempts at contacting them have gone unanswered. Last anyone heard, the geologists who made the video were going to try to find the point of impact where this object came down. We have no idea whether they found it or what happened to them."

"Isn't this how the movie *Aliens* started?" Brighton asked. "With a space colony suddenly cutting off communication after a UFO crash landing?"

Paxton rolled his eyes. "Lost Aspen's pretty new, and it's in the middle of Antarctica," he said. "It could just be a simple technical failure."

"You have zero imagination, man," Brighton said. "You're going to be the first one the monster eats. Well... after me, anyway." Several of the men laughed.

"These are our orders," Cross continued as if he had never been interrupted in the first place. "Locate the crashed object, bring it back for study, figure out why the research station stopped communicating, and make sure the civilians are safe. Stealth is going to be of paramount importance on this one. Nobody has any territorial claims on Marie Byrd Land, but no country is supposed to be sending troops on missions anywhere in Antarctica, either."

"Are we expecting anyone else to be breaking that rule besides us, Commander?" Yamashita asked.

"It's possible," Cross said. "If this object is man-made, whoever made it is probably going to come looking for it. And any other government that attached the same significance to the video that ours did will send people, too. No specific intel has been confirmed yet, but we've heard whispers of Russian Special Forces on the scene."

"Seems like the longer the video's out there, the more likely we're going to have company," Yamashita said.

"About that," Cross said. "Phantom Cell's running a psy-ops campaign in support of our efforts. They're simultaneously spreading the word that the video's a hoax and doing their best to stop it from spreading by eliminating circulation."

"Good luck to them on that last one," Brighton

said. "You can't stop the Internet. Phantom Cell's good, but nobody's *that* good."

"Not our concern," Cross said. "We ship out in one hour, so get your gear on the Commando. We'll go over more mission specifics during the flight. Understood?"

"Sir," the men responded in unison. At a nod from Cross, they rose and gathered up the remains of their breakfasts. As they left the briefing room, Walker remained behind. He gulped down the last of his coffee before standing up.

"Brighton's sure excited," Walker said.

"I knew he would be," Cross replied. "I didn't expect him to try to help out so much with the briefing, though."

Walker hesitated for a moment. "Is that what I'm like whenever I chip in from up here?" he asked.

Cross fought off the urge to toy with his second-in-command, but he couldn't stop a mischievous smile from creeping across his face. "Maybe a little bit," he said.

Walker returned Cross's grin. "Then I wholeheartedly apologize," he said.

INTEL

DECRYPTING

12345

COM CHATTER

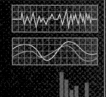

- AHKIO: sled used to carry things
- CAVALIER: if you are cavalier, you show a lack of proper concern for something
- SHORTS: ski-shoes used for traversing snow and ice
- UAV: unmanned aerial vehicle, or a drone

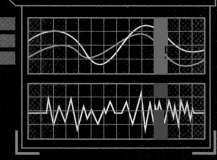

3245.98

CHAPTER TWO

1324.014

PARALLEL SUNS

After several monotonous hours of flying in the MC130-J Commando II plane, Shadow Squadron made a single stop to transfer to a CH-53E Super Stallion transport helicopter. A few hours more, and the team was finally at its destination.

The blank, unbroken expanse of Marie Byrd Land, Antarctica, stretched out below. Half of the ground was obscured by cloud cover and glare from the sun.

As Cross peered down the horizon, he saw what looked like two parallel suns. "Am I hallucinating?" he asked, pointing at the strange sight.

Brighton answered him. "No, sir," he said excitedly. "That's a phantom sun. It's a phenomenon that occurs when sunlight is refracted through ice crystals. Pretty cool, if you ask me." Brighton nudged Yamashita in the ribs. "Kinda looks like a sniper scope's reticule, huh?"

"No," Yamashita answered flatly. He shot Cross an annoyed look.

"I'm sorry I asked," Cross said with a chuckle. Brighton was usually pretty excited on missions, but he seemed to be especially enthusiastic about this one.

As the Super Stallion began its descent, Cross clapped once to get his men's attention. "I know you've all been through Pickel Meadows and Kodiak and Black Rapids," he said, referring to the Marines', Navy's, and Army's respective northern and mountain training centers. "But this isn't going to be exactly like that. For one thing, it's actually summer right now in Antarctica. Temperatures could get up to a balmy 60 out on the coast — a little colder inland where we are. For another, it's not going to get dark. At all. The sun won't set down here for another month at least. That means you won't be able to rely on it for direction, either. Also, remember what Williams said about whiteout and snow blindness — keep your sunglasses on at all times when we're outdoors."

WHUMP!

The helicopter thumped down hard onto the thickly packed Antarctic ice. Cross supervised his team's last-minute gear checks, then ordered the flight crew to lower the rear cargo hatch.

WOOOOOOSH!

Frigid wind clawed its way into the cargo bay, easily overpowering the wall-mounted space heaters. Cross couldn't help but check to make sure everyone was properly bundled in their cold-weather gear.

"Commander?" Yamashita called, drawing Cross's attention back to the cargo ramp. The sniper stood at the top, facing down and outside toward something Cross couldn't see. His voice had the same tone of guarded caution Cross heard when Yamashita was waiting for the go-ahead to take a shot with his M110 rifle.

Cross walked over to Yamashita and found him staring at a stranger standing midway up the ramp with his hands out at both sides. The stranger wasn't dressed in a military-issue, seven-layer Extended Cold Weather Clothing System (or ECWCS) like the members of Cross's team. Nor was he dressed like the airfield skeleton crew Cross could see coming toward the plane from farther off to refuel it. This man's winter gear was all expensive, store-brand stuff that might as well have had the price tags still attached for how new it all looked.

Cross tilted his head as an introduction, wondering if the man was some civilian scientist who'd accidentally wandered into a place he shouldn't be.

"Lieutenant Commander Ryan Cross, I presume?" the stranger asked. He grinned. "Permission to come aboard, sir?"

"Who are you and what are you doing out here?" Cross demanded. The tone of the stranger's voice and the smug confidence in his grin reminded Cross of himself when he was much younger. It was an unpleasant mirror to gaze into.

"Bill Dyer," the man said. "From Phantom Cell. I've been assigned to your squadron for the duration of this mission."

"So you say," Cross replied. "How'd you get here so fast?" The men behind Cross read the tension in his body language and stopped to watch how things would play out.

Dyer's grin widened. "I was already on assignment not far from here," he said. "I hitched a ride with the ground crew."

"I'll have to confirm this with Command," Cross said.

"Sure, sure," Dyer said amiably.

Cross turned and headed back toward the helicopter's cockpit, giving Yamashita a look as he turned. Yamashita nodded his understanding and remained in Cross's place to glare at Dyer.

Picking up on the hint, Dyer strolled down the ramp and stood out of the way as Shadow Squadron continued to unload gear.

A quick call back to Command confirmed Dyer's story and earned Cross an apology for the slow communication. He informed his men of the change in plans and approached Dyer once more.

"You're legit," Cross said. "Sorry about that."

"No harm done," Dyer said, as if Cross hadn't kept him waiting. "And welcome to Pluto." That joke drew a chuckle from Brighton.

Cross looked around. The outpost where they'd landed extended into a blue-ice runway that continued for miles until it disappeared from sight. There were also two drab, pre-fabricated, semi-cylindrical buildings that were partially buried in snow and ice. They looked like giant cans that'd been dropped carelessly into the ground.

"Camp's not much to look at," Dyer said, noticing Cross's skepticism. "It's been abandoned for a few years since the Pine Island Glacier camp opened up. That one's a little more central and convenient to the stations that use it. We still had this place on record, though, and figured it would serve as a nice out-of-the-way base of operations. The ground crew cleaned the place out and got it up and running. In another few weeks, it might actually be warm in the main building. I wouldn't hold my breath, though."

Cross nodded for him to continue.

"The good news is," Dyer said, "I've been able to pinpoint the crash site you're here to find. It's only a dozen or so miles away, between us and Lost Aspen. I figure we should go ahead and check out the crash site first."

"How did you find it?" Brighton asked.

"It wasn't too hard," Dyer said with a cavalier shrug. "I'm the one who caused the crash, after all."

Stunned silence followed that claim. Cross was the first to break it. "Come again?"

"Yeah, what is it?" Brighton asked.

"It's a hunter-killer drone satellite," Dyer explained. "Think of it like an orbital UAV. I caught it trying to hack into one of our spy satellites and engaged in a tug-of-war with its operator. I locked him out and stole it from him, but I couldn't keep it from crashing."

"Who built it?" Brighton asked with childlike fascination.

"Probably the Chinese," Dyer said. "Regardless, the operator was definitely Chinese. I've crossed swords with him a few times, so to speak. I was able to blind him from where the drone crashed, so we've got a head start. But it's only going to be a matter of time before they figure that Internet video out and come looking, so we need to get to the site in a hurry."

"All right," Cross said, annoyed with the way the Phantom Cell operative casually gave orders as if he were in charge. "As soon as the snowmobiles are ready and we get our gear set up, we'll head out there and check it out."

Dyer winced. "Actually, Commander, I was just coming to that," he said. "Snowmobiles might not be an option right now — unless you've got some of those Canadian stealth jobs."

"Canada has stealth snowmobiles?" Walker asked, his tone doubtful.

"Yeah, they're pretty cool, Chief," Brighton said. "They're hybrid-electric with like a 150-mile range. They can get up to, like, 50 miles per hour. I think they call them..." He looked back and forth between Walker and Cross, neither of whom looked glad for his input. "Anyway, they're neat."

"Edgar Brighton," Dyer said, extending a hand. "It's a pleasure. Bill Dyer, Phantom Cell. We heard about what you did with the Avenger drone over Saraqeb. Impressive stuff."

"Thanks, man!" Brighton said, shaking Dyer's hand. If Brighton was at all disappointed to find that the object that had crashed wasn't an alien spaceship, he didn't show it. "Sounds kind of like what you did with this satellite drone thing."

Dyer winked. "Like I said, Impressive."

"What's this about not using the snowmobiles?" Cross cut in.

"We'll talk later, when you've got a minute," Dyer said to Brighton. To Cross, he said, "Silence is going to be golden on this one, Commander. The Chinese might not know where to look for their drone yet, but the Russians are already on the case. They landed a team a few hours before you guys got here."

"Are they scientists?" Chief Walker asked.

"Nope," Dyer said. "My information indicates they're Spetsnaz. I think they're responsible for the communications blackout from Lost Aspen. No confirmation on that intel, though."

"Russian Special Forces," Cross said. "Could be worse, I guess. We're not technically enemies with them anymore."

"Just calling them Spetsnaz doesn't tell us much," Walker said. "You know anything more about the specific unit in play?"

Dyer shook his head. "Wish I did," he said. "But

according to radio intercepts, they're definitely Russian and definitely here because of the video. They're ahead of us, but I can't say if they've found the site or not. They cut me off before I could learn more."

"Regardless, they're out there right now," Cross said. "Watching, listening, and with no more right to be here than we have. You're correct — we can't risk a noisy approach."

"Plus," Dyer added, "if they know that you know they're here, they'll go to some lengths to make sure you don't tell anybody. You know, since none of us are supposed to be here at all."

"Possibly," Walker said.

"It's something you guys should be considering as well," Dyer said. "I mean, as soon as they know we're here, it might be wise to..."

"No," Cross said. "That isn't how we operate. If operational security becomes a problem, we'll deal with it in due time. The Russians aren't my main concern, though — the scientists are. Making sure they are safe is our top priority."

"With respect, Commander," Dyer said, "the drone is the top priority."

"That's what it says on our orders," Cross said. "But I'm in charge here, and I decide what's most important. If you don't like that, you can take it up with Command."

"Duly noted," Dyer said neutrally.

"In any event," Cross continued, "the crash site's between us and Lost Aspen. We'll stop by there to see what we can see on the way. Got it?"

"I'm just an observer and technical advisor," Dyer said with a shrug. "You guys are the ones with the weapons. We'll do it your way."

"All right then," Cross said. He turned away to address his men. They quickly gathered around to listen. "We've confirmed there's a rival team on the field: Russian Special Forces — we don't know how many. They've got a head start, but we don't know how much of one. I don't need to remind you of the sticky legal situation our being here represents. Suffice it to say, this operation just went from top-secret to full black. That means total noise discipline en route. We're leaving the snowmobiles behind and going out on the shorts. We'll recon the crash site and secure it if we're first on the scene, then radio back for the Super Stallion. I want you to finish unloading your gear, stretch your legs, change your socks, carb up, and hydrate. Then load up your ahkios because we're leaving in twenty minutes."

"Sir," the men responded.

When Cross finished, Dyer looked at him and pretended to cough behind his hand.

"Right, one more thing," Cross said. "This is Bill Dyer of Phantom Cell. He's coming with us as an advisor. He's the reason we're here, so I need a volunteer to buddy up and keep an eye on him."

"Can you ski?" Shepherd asked with a skeptical frown. "Or shoot? Did you even bring a gun?"

"Yes to all three," Dyer said. "My rifle's with the rest of my gear. And yeah, I can ski and shoot. I was an alternate on the '94 Olympic men's biathlon team."

Paxton smirked. "Didn't the Russians take home the most gold in biathlon that year?" he asked.

"Only because I didn't get to compete against them," Dyer assured him.

"Thank you for volunteering, Sergeant," Cross said to Paxton. "Make sure Dyer and his gear are ready to go when we are."

"Sir," Paxton said.

"Twenty minutes, people," Cross reiterated to the whole team. "Get started."

5514.108

INTEL

DECRYPTING

12345

COM CHATTER

- GPS: global positioning system, or an electronic system that uses satellites to determine one's position
- INFRARED: in terms of optics, infrared vision lets the viewer see heat signatures
- M110: an American-made, semi-automatic sniper rifle

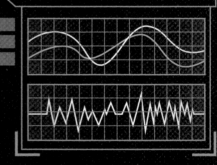

3245.98

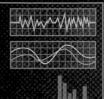

OPTICS

The first leg of Shadow Squadron's journey to the crash site proceeded without incident. The team set out on their shorts, which combined the best features of skis and snowshoes. The carbon fiber ski-shoes offered a wide, flat base for moving over loose powder or uphill. They also had a set of corrugated scales beneath the soles of the soldiers' boots which offered traction without inhibiting forward motion.

Dyer was geared similarly, but once again his equipment was top-of-the-line professional sports gear rather than the field-tested special order equipment Shadow Squadron soldiers used.

As they traveled, the soldiers wore their seven-layer ECWCS outfits with digital white-blue-gray camouflage. They carried their rifles on their backs. The rest of their gear they dragged behind them in lightweight carbon fiber ahkio sleds attached to harnesses on their belts. The only exception in this case was Dyer, who had only brought a heavy backpack and had no sled.

The sun and its double looped through the sky, flirting with the horizon but never quite touching it. Cross resisted the urge to go all the way to the crash site immediately. He was concerned that the lack of a regular day-and-night cycle would cause him to accidentally push his men too hard and wear them out early. When his compass and GPS told him the team was still a couple of miles from the crash site, he ordered them to stop and make camp.

The men dug down several feet through the ice and snow and set up tents along with an electric field stove. Then the team ate and took turns resting for the long trip to follow.

Although Dyer had stayed by Paxton's side

for the whole trip thus far, Cross noticed that the Phantom Cell operative had barely said a word to the Green Beret once camp was set up. Instead, Dyer spent most of his time talking to Brighton, praising the short-range Four-Eyes UAV drone that Brighton had designed. Then he went on to engage him in a discussion of computing and surveillance technology that sounded more like science fiction speculation to Cross than anything with real-world applications. Then again, Cross hadn't been able to imagine anything like smartphones or UAV drones when he'd first joined the Navy, but those things were everywhere now.

Since the pair of them were getting along so well, Cross reassigned Brighton to keep an eye on Dyer, which suited both men just fine. Paxton privately admitted to being relieved as well after Cross informed him of the switch. Paxton couldn't explain exactly why, but something about Dyer rubbed him the wrong way. Cross didn't respond to Paxton's concern, but his impression of Dyer was much the same. The man had an air of competence and charisma about him, but it was an oily sort of charisma. A youthful kind of cockiness that flew in the face of caution for the sake of success.

"That could be it," Chief Walker said after Cross expressed his concerns. "Or it could be you're just getting old, Commander. Same stuff comes to mind when I think about you most days." Walker tried to hide his smirk behind his tin coffee cup.

"I see," Cross said. "Thanks for that, Chief."

"Anytime, sir."

Some hours later, the soldiers broke camp and set out in silence once again. They made remarkable time, moving primarily downhill over smooth terrain. Well before lunchtime, they topped a small hill, which gave them their first view of the site where the drone had crashed.

Cross called everyone to a stop. The men gathered up around him. "This is the place," he said. "And it's right where you said it would be, Dyer. Good work."

"Math," Dyer replied with a shrug of humility. Cross didn't buy it.

The site itself wasn't all that impressive. The impact crater was comet-shaped where the drone had come in at a shallow angle. It had melted a trail and gouged a hole in the frozen landscape. Cottony diamond dust settled low over the area, making the air sparkle.

"Binoculars," Cross said. "Glass and FLIR. Let's take a look around before we get down there."

The soldiers drew their ahkios in close and kneeled over their ski-shoes to examine the crash site with regular field binoculars and forward-looking infrared (or FLIR) binoculars. Dyer got down beside Brighton and scanned the area with a single-lens FLIR spyglass.

Yamashita kicked out of his ski-shoes to lie prone at the crest of the hill. He lay looking casually over the area with the Leupold scope on his M110 sniper rifle. A taut mesh of loose-weave white nylon covered the end of his scope, though it didn't seem to obscure his vision. "No wreckage," Yamashita said.

"No scientists, either," Walker added, peering

through one of the sets of FLIR binoculars. "Or Russians."

"I see tracks," Cross said. "Snowmobile tracks back and forth on the far side. The ones leading out have a heavy trench behind and between them. They don't look that fresh. Probably from the geologists. There are ski tracks too that come in from a different angle. Looks like they head off in the direction the snowmobiles came from. They're fresher, too."

"They're probably from the Russians," Walker said. "Tracking the geologists."

"*Hunting* them," Dyer corrected.

"If my read's right," Cross said, "the scientists in the video found this site, attached the drone to their snowmobiles, and then dragged it back to Lost Aspen. Sometime later, the Russians showed up and followed the trail back. They could be at Lost Aspen already."

"They almost certainly are," Dyer said. "It's time to consider a full —"

Cross was about to set Dyer straight on who was giving the orders when the ground several feet down the hill in front of them suddenly sprayed a double-handful of snow in the air.

FOOSH!

Cross flinched and watched the tiny white flakes drift back to earth.

"What the heck?" Dyer asked, looking just as surprised as Cross felt.

FOOSH!!

Another puff of snow shot up in front of Walker's feet. "Sniper!" Yamashita hissed, figuring it out at the same time Cross did. "Sniper — find cover!"

Cross and Walker dove backward, hoping to put the crest of their small hill between themselves and the shooter. Brighton, meanwhile, lurched out of his ski-shoes to tackle Dyer to the ground.

CRACK!!!

A sharp noise broke the eerie silence of the attack. Both Brighton and Dyer yelped in surprise and pain as they landed in a tangle of arms and legs and rolled down the hill, bumping awkwardly over Dyer's bulky backpack. Williams, the team's medic, popped out of his ski-shoes and crawl-slid over to them to check for injuries.

"Sleds up!" Cross ordered, yanking his ahkio up beside him where he lay, hauling it one-handed toward the hilltop.

The others began to do the same, balancing their sleds on edge in the snow, using the weight of the gear strapped on top of the sleds to keep them balanced upright. They lined up the ahkios in a crooked line that looked like the tops of a medieval castle wall, then they hunkered down behind them. The advanced carbon fiber skin over the lightweight metal core of the sleds made them somewhat bullet resistant, if not bulletproof. In any case, the sleds offered better cover than the snowy nothingness all around them.

With the quick-and-dirty wall erected, Cross motioned for the others to move back down the hill away from it and slide over to the left. While he'd seen video of the sleds stopping small-arms fire, he didn't want to test his luck against a high-powered sniper rifle. He also didn't want the sniper to get lucky by arcing his shots over the makeshift wall. When the others were relocated, only Yamashita remained on the line, lying exactly where he'd been the whole time. He hadn't flinched at the signs of gunfire, nor had he moved his sled into line with the others. He just lay perfectly still, looking downrange through his Leupold scope with the patience of a stone.

Cross came to check on Brighton and Dyer. "They're all right, Commander," Williams said. "No blood, no foul. Neither one of them was hit."

"Jerk blew up my binoculars," Brighton said. He sat up and showed Cross the remains of the black-and-gray FLIR lenses. They had been dangling around his neck from a long nylon lanyard when he'd tackled the Phantom Cell operative to pull him to safety. The binoculars now had a small hole on one side where the bullet had gone in and an enormous blossom of twisted metal and plastic on the other side where the bullet had exited.

"I swear to you, he will pay for that," Dyer said with all the gravity of a Shakespearean actor. "He. Will. Pay."

Brighton snickered and punched Dyer in the shoulder.

"Stay down," Cross told the two of them. To Williams he said, "Which one of the sleds is yours?"

"Far left," Williams said, nodding at the sled closest to Yamashita. "Why?"

"Could be important," Cross said. "I just hope it isn't."

Without further explanation, Cross crawled back up the hill to the ahkio wall and opened Williams' gear. He dug out a medical bag and slid it back down the hill to where the medic lay waiting. Next, he picked up a pair of FLIR binoculars and edged toward the first gap in the sled wall, hoping to determine where the enemy sniper was hiding.

"Don't," Yamashita said calmly. "He'll see the glare."

He has a point, Cross realized. The sun was behind the opposing sniper, shining in Cross's eyes. In fact, it was so bitterly cold and clear that phantom suns shone to the right and left of the actual sun, giving the entire bleak landscape the look of an alien planet. Thanks to Brighton's excited explanation earlier, Cross now knew that the phantom suns were just optical illusions created by ice crystals. But that fact didn't make the sight seem any less creepy under the circumstances.

Regardless, the light was more than bright enough to cast a glare off the lenses of his binoculars and give his position away. Fortunately, the nylon mesh over the end of Yamashita's rifle scope prevented that from happening to him.

"Do you see him?" Cross whispered to Yamashita.

"I haven't fired yet, sir," Yamashita replied. "I've got eyes on a couple of likely spots, but he hasn't obliged me by moving or shooting again."

"Think we can slip behind where you think he is?" Cross asked.

"Not if he's any good," Yamashita said.

"If he were any good, he would have hit at least one of us with those first three shots," Cross argued.

"That wasn't for lack of skill," Yamashita said. "It's a problem with optics in terrain like this. Things in the distance look bigger and closer than they really are since everything is one color. It just took him a couple of shots to adjust for difference. The fact he didn't get a kill on his third shot was pure dumb luck."

"I see," Cross said, unsettled by how close Brighton and Dyer both had apparently come to death. "This is your game. What's our next move?"

"If you can get him to shoot again without getting yourself killed, I'll take it from there, Commander," Yamashita said. He paused for a second and then added, "Well, either way... When he shoots, I can take him out."

"My soul will rest easy knowing that," Cross murmured. "Okay, hang tight. I've got an idea."

Moving carefully and hoping not to draw the enemy sniper's attention, Cross picked up the binoculars he'd been about to use. Then he rolled as fast as he could across the first gap in the sled wall to where the next two sleds sat end to end. His heart raced, fearing that the sniper would see the sudden motion and put a one-in-a-million shot through the gap. When no shot came, his heart kept racing, anyway. Cross also feared that the sniper saw the roll but was just patiently lining up a kill shot that would punch through the shield wall and into him. After another few eternally long, pulse-pounding seconds, Cross's fears dimmed to nearly nothing.

Pulling his fur-lined cap off from beneath his jacket's hood, Cross laid it down on top of the binoculars he'd grabbed. These he laid on the curved underside of one of the ski-shoes Paxton had kicked off when the warning had gone out.

Then, lying on his back behind the first of the two adjacent sleds, he used the ski-shoe to lift the hat and binoculars ever-so-slowly up over the top edge of the second sled. When it was just high enough, he propped it up on the side of the sled. His hope was that the lenses of the binoculars would cast a glare and attract the enemy sniper's attention, and that the silhouette of the hat and binoculars would look like a soldier peering up over the top of the wall —

CRACK!!!

At first, Cross didn't realize what had happened. One second he was looking up at his decoy and wondering how long it would take for the sniper to take the bait. A split-second later, the binoculars exploded as a bullet punched right through them. The hat went flying and a piece of the binoculars snapped off and flew past Cross's face, nicking his cheek.

At what seemed like the same instant, a muted cough came from Yamashita's rifle.

CRUCK.

Less than a second later, the sickening sound of impact came back from the opposite end of the crash site.

"Clear," Yamashita said. His voice was quiet and subdued, but he didn't whisper.

Cross pressed a hand to his cheek. His mitten came away with a thin, short line of blood from where the bit of shrapnel had cut him. "You sure you got him?"

Yamashita gave a small shudder that only Cross was close enough to see. "I have eyes on the target now, Commander," he said. "I got him." He said the last three words so quietly they almost disappeared in the icy wind.

"Does he have a spotter?" Cross asked. He knew Yamashita well enough by now to know not to thank him or praise the quality of his shooting.

"No," Yamashita replied.

"Must have been a sentry," Cross speculated. "Probably radioed in as soon as he saw us."

"I would have," Yamashita agreed.

Cross frowned. "That means either reinforcements are coming, or they're going to be holed up waiting for us when we get to Lost Aspen."

"Either way, we don't have much time to wait around, sir," Yamashita said.

Cross nodded. "Gear up and get your shorts back on. Take your partner and head up the path. Scout the way and find out what you can. We'll join you shortly."

"Sir," Yamashita said. He waved downhill to get Jannati's attention and signaled the Marine to join him. They paired up and Yamashita explained Cross's orders. Jannati nodded and got his gear together.

Cross descended the hill to address the remaining men. "Sniper's down," he began, "but it's more than likely the enemy knows we're here and figures we're on the way. They're either going to meet us halfway or dig in and let us come to them."

"And they're probably going to start executing the civilians," Dyer said under his breath. "So there are no witnesses."

"You'll speak when I ask for your opinion," Cross snapped at him.

Dyer flinched. "Sir, yessir," he drawled. His tone was low and flippant, but he broke eye contact under the force of Cross's unwavering glare.

"Gear up," Cross said to his men. "We're moving out."

INTEL

DECRYPTING

12345

COM CHATTER

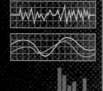

- BALACLAVA: mask that covers the entire head and face except for the eyes and nose (and sometimes the mouth)
- AN-94: a Russian-made assault rifle
- VSS VINTOREZ: a Russian-made, quiet sniper rifle

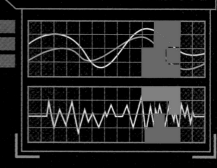

3245.98

CHAPTER FOUR

COMRADE

To give Yamashita and Jannati time to move ahead and scout, Cross led his men over to the dead Russian sniper for a quick examination. What was left of him wasn't very helpful. The man carried no ID papers or personal mementos. The only equipment he had was a pack of energy bars, a two-way earpiece radio, a VSS Vintorez sniper rifle, and half a dozen magazines for it.

Only Cross had the stomach to remove the sniper's earpiece and dig the radio out of his coat. He looped the earpiece over his ear, opposite the one in which his own canalphone nestled. A double-pop of static indicated a signal from the sniper's comrades. Cross repeated the signal with taps on the transmitting part of the earpiece. One more pop came over the line, then a wary Russian voice spoke a single phrase.

Without pressing the earpiece to transmit, Cross looked at Walker. "Sub-shot?" he asked, repeating the Russian he'd heard as best he could repeat it. "What's that mean, Chief? Or it might have been sub-shet..."

"Report," Walker replied.

When Cross didn't answer, the voice spoke again.

"Sh-toe shloo-chee-less?" Cross relayed. "K-toe ah-nee?"

"'What happened?' maybe," Walker said. "Then, 'Who are they?' Sir, if you want me to try to talk to —"

"I've got it," Cross said.

After a long pause, Cross still did not reply. In response, the radio clicked one more time and then

fell silent. Cross cocked an eyebrow in thought, feeling every eye on him. He looked at Walker, then at Dyer before he spoke.

"How many people are stationed at Lost Aspen?" he asked.

"Forty-one," Dyer said. "Assuming your Spetsnaz counterparts haven't —"

Cross cut Dyer off with a hard glare. Then he tapped the dead Russian's radio earpiece, opening the channel.

"I know you can hear me," Cross said softly into the radio. "You and I need to talk. Sooner rather than later."

"What are you doing?" Dyer hissed. His eyes widened so much that his eyebrows completely cleared the tops of his too-expensive mirrored shades.

"Sir..." Walker said.

"Kto eto?" a flat voice said from the other end of the Russian radio frequency. It wasn't the same one that had spoken before.

"I'm going to assume," Cross said, "that you just asked me either who I am or what I want. Is that right?"

"Da," the Russian replied. Then under a heavy accent, "Yes — the first. Who are you?"

"Does it matter?" Cross asked.

"Nyet. Not really."

"So ask me what you really want to know."

"My soldier," the Russian said. "You have him?"

"No," Cross said. "He fired on us. He's dead."

The Russian made no reply for almost a minute. Cross desperately hoped the man was simply composing himself rather than ordering his men to start executing scientists. When he finally spoke again, his voice was as flat and emotionless as before. "You have any casualties?"

"No," Cross said.

"How many men are with you?" he asked.

Cross smirked. "Enough to get the job done. You?"

"More than plenty," the Russian said. "Though now one less."

"Let me bring you his remains," Cross said, causing Walker and Dyer to flinch in surprise. "This is no fit place for a soldier to rest."

"That's... an unexpected offer," the voice said. "You would do this?"

"Yes," Cross said. "In exchange for a chance to talk."

"And what have we to talk about?" he asked.

"I'd say we have 41 things left yet to talk about," Cross said. "Or 42, if you count the real reason we were both sent here."

"Indeed," the Russian said. "Very well. Bring the body to the end of the trail. We will speak there, you and I. Only you and I."

"Understood," Cross said. "Out."

He tapped the Russian earpiece one last time and removed it from his ear. Before Walker or Dyer could start in on him, Cross double-tapped his own canalphone.

"Commander?" Yamashita replied, his voice barely above a whisper.

"I take it you're in position," Cross said. "You have eyes on Lost Aspen?"

"Sir."

"Any sign of the scientists?"

"Not unless they use AN-94s in their research," Yamashita said. "If they do, then I count nine 'scientists.' Four on top of the station, two at the main door of the flag-section — that'll make sense when you see this place — and three standing guard over something wrapped up tight in white tarps. Probably the drone. Orders, sir?"

"Hang tight and don't give yourselves away," Cross said. "We're going to move up in a few minutes, then I'm going down to Lost Aspen alone to have a chat."

"Sir," Yamashita replied.

Cross turned to address the rest of Shadow Squadron as they gathered around him. "All right, here's what I want you all to do..."

* * *

It took Cross only a few minutes to unload his ahkio then wrap and place the dead Russian sniper on it. But in that time, he got an earful from both Walker and Dyer about his plan. Walker was at least respectful enough to keep his opinion pitched low so the rest of the men didn't hear, but Dyer objected loudly and repeatedly. Neither of them could see what Cross hoped to gain by going into the lion's den alone, even if the rest of the team was watching in silence from nearby. While Cross respected Walker's opinion, it didn't help the Chief's case that Dyer agreed with him.

But Cross was determined to take this route. So, once the rest of the team had moved up without him, Cross came sliding up to Lost Aspen all alone, pulling a corpse on a sled behind him.

Cross noticed that Lost Aspen itself was gorgeous. Based on a group of British architects' genius design plans, the facility resembled an enormous metal centipede on skis. It consisted of seven house-sized modules rising over 20 feet off the snow on sets of four hydraulic struts functioning as broad-flat skis. Each module connected to the one behind by way of a flexible, accordion-like hallway. Six of the modules were painted glossy green. The center module was the largest of the seven, and it had been painted in a wrap-around American flag so that the blue star-field spilled over the top and the red and white stripes wrapped around the underside. Cross had read about the British Halley VI Antarctic Research Station on which the design of Lost Aspen had been modeled. If the designs were as similar as they looked, that meant the flag section was the communal and entertainment center for the facility.

Two guards stood posted by the main door of the flag section, just as Yamashita had reported. A quick glance around revealed seven more sentinels more or less where he had expected them. These soldiers wore layered cold-weather gear in gray-and-white camouflage print. They carried AN-94 assault rifles, and their faces were obscured by white balaclavas.

Two soldiers waited beside the tarp-wrapped

remains of the downed orbital drone. Cross spared it a glance before turning his attention to the lone figure who approached him across the ice on cleated boots.

"Here we go," Cross murmured, barely moving his lips. The comm channel remained open through the canalphone in his ear.

The Russian stopped ten feet from Cross and looked him over, his rifle in his hands but aimed at nothing. Unlike the others, he had taken his balaclava off. His face was hard-set and lined. His eyes were blue-green pools, shimmering with equal parts caution and cunning. He made no effort to hide his suspicion.

"You are he?" the Russian said. It was the same one Cross had spoken to on the radio.

Cross nodded. He gestured at the ahkio behind him. "I am. And I've brought your man."

The Russian stepped forward and extended a gloved hand, keeping his other hand on his rifle. "Give me the lead," he said.

"First let's talk about what you've got under that tarp," Cross said.

"The satellite?" the Russian said. He gestured at the science facility behind him. "Perhaps you want to talk about what's wrapped inside that garish flag first."

Cross caught his meaning and nodded. "Yes, the scientists," he said. "They're American citizens."

"As are you, I think," the Russian said. "Unless that's a Canadian accent I am hearing."

"They're civilians," Cross said. "They've got nothing to do with this. Out of all of us, they're the only ones with any right to be here."

The Russian cocked his head and peered at Cross stone-faced. "Ask me what you really want to know."

"Are they dead?" Cross asked flatly.

"No."

Cross was barely able to conceal his surprise. "No? Then what are your intentions toward them?"

"I was prepared to live and let live," the Russian replied. "They need never have known we were here."

This time, Cross couldn't hide his surprise. "Come again?" he asked.

"We incapacitated them with a sleeping agent administered through the ventilation system," the Russian said.

"Like in the Dubrovka theater?" Cross asked, his blood running cold. Spetsnaz soldiers had used a similar tactic some years ago to subdue terrorists who'd taken a theater full of civilians hostage in Moscow. While the terrorists had been defeated once the gas took effect, more than 100 hostages died from adverse reactions to that gas.

"That was the work of thugs," the Russian said, scowling. "No finesse. Besides, that was a decade ago." He took a deep breath, and his face returned to its neutral expression. "No, right now, the biggest risk to these people's safety is you and your men."

"How do you figure?" Cross asked.

"It is my understanding that your military does not negotiate over hostages in situations such as this," he said. "Especially not on your illegal 'black ops,' yes?"

"That's not my policy," Cross said. "Personally I don't care what's under that tarp. I want to know my people are all right. I'll do whatever it takes to make sure of it."

The Russian blinked in surprise. "You are not here for the satellite, then?" he said.

"It's a secondary objective," Cross said. "Frankly, if what you're saying is true, you can walk away with it right now."

"Then I assure you it is true," the Russian said. His words rolled out slowly, as if his mind couldn't process what Cross said. "You have my word."

Cross smirked. "Give me some credit for common sense. What's that old saying? 'Trust but verify.'"

The Russian cracked a smile. "As you wish. If you will come with me..."

"I'll just wait here, thanks," Cross said. He turned his head to the side and said, "All right, Sergeant. Four Eyes is a 'go.' Check things out in the middle section of the facility."

Cross turned his attention back to the Russian. "Tell your men to leave the door open," he said.

At Cross's order, Brighton remotely activated the Four Eyes UAV quad-copter that had sat unnoticed on the ahkio sled between the dead sniper's boots. The UAV hummed to life and rose to shoulder height behind Cross.

"Sir," Brighton said over Cross's canalphone.

"*Krúto,*" the Russian murmured with an impressed look on his face.

"It's just a camera platform," Cross said as the UAV buzzed past him and began to slowly move toward Lost Aspen. "No weapons, no explosives."

The Russian ordered the guards at the flag module to open the doors, and one of them went inside with the UAV. Several long moments later, Brighton's voice sounded in Cross's canalphone.

"All the civilians are accounted for, sir," Brighton said. "Looks like they're all sleeping."

"Sir," Williams cut in. "They're all alive and they appear to be unconscious. I can't say more without a proper examination, but it looks like they're all right."

"Okay," Cross said, both to his men and to the Russian. "I'm satisfied."

The Russian nodded. Brighton piloted the UAV back out of the flag module and landed it next to Cross.

"All right then," Cross said. "If you and your men are willing to leave without giving us any trouble, you can take your prize and go. I'll be happy to remember we never saw you."

"And we likewise," the Russian said. His tone and expression remained wary, as if he believed he was being tricked. "Now, if I may..."

Once more, he extended a hand, palm up, reaching for the lead to the ahkio sled with his comrade's body on it. This time, Cross met him halfway and handed the lead over.

The Russian pulled the sled over to him and knelt beside it. He grabbed a corner of the covering Cross had used as a shroud. After a brief hesitation, he peeled it back. The man winced at the condition of the body that lay revealed. The Russian's shoulders sagged for a moment, but he was all business by the time he re-covered his fallen comrade and stood to face Cross once again.

"We didn't expect anyone else to get here so quickly," the Russian said, staring out at the endless white horizon. "I only ordered him to watch over the crash site to get him out of my hair for a while." He sighed, and his eyes focused on Cross's once more. "Thank you for bringing him back."

Cross gave no reply. There was nothing he could say that the Russian would have wanted to hear.

"Now, we have preparations to make. Our Mi-8 will be here within the hour. I suggest you withdraw to wherever the rest of your men are hiding until we are gone. I do not want to have to explain your presence." He glanced down at the ahkio again. "I suspect I shall have more than enough to answer for."

"You and me both, Comrade," Cross said.

INTEL

DECRYPTING

12345

COM CHATTER

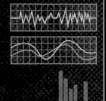

- DRONE: a pilotless aircraft often controlled via remote
- CONSPIRACY THEORY: a belief based on questionable evidence that a group, like the government, is behind a secret or plot

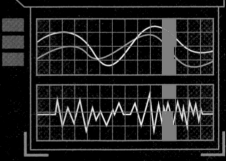

3245.98

CHAPTER FIVE

1324.014

COLD LIGHT

Cross and his team regrouped at Lost Aspen. Williams, Chief Walker, and Paxton were looking after the scientists now that they'd regained consciousness. No one seemed to be suffering any ill effects from whatever chemical the Russians had used on them, but a fleet of rescue helicopters had been called in to evacuate everyone as a precaution.

In the meantime, the scientists were starting to ask questions. Dyer set to work, feeding them the simple cover story he'd made up. According to him, the US military had sent in the Marines to investigate after communication with the research

station had suddenly ceased. The soldiers had found everyone sleeping peacefully in the facility with no indication of what had happened to them. He pretended to be completely confused when they asked questions about the strange object they had recovered from the meteorite crash site. He repeated over and over that there was no evidence of any such object at the site or anywhere near Lost Aspen.

When the scientists grew more insistent, Dyer simply asked them about the object, knowing full-well that none of them could tell him anything specific since even the four scientists from the video who'd recovered it had only a vague idea of what it was. They knew it was metal and that it was man-made. Beyond that, they couldn't recall anything. And the more Dyer questioned them and worked them over, the less certain they became of the object's existence.

Cross had to admit that Dyer was good at his job. By confusing their memories of the event, he'd made their claims too insufficient for even a conspiracy theory.

After the last of the scientists were evacuated, Dyer had a brief conversation with Brighton, then left. Cross was debating the best way to ask about the discussion when Brighton approached him.

"I can't believe you just gave that device to the Russians, man," Brighton said.

"Command's not going to be happy," Cross admitted, "but I stand by my decision. I'd do it again if given the same opportunity."

"Well, sure, but what if it had been something from outer space?" Brighton asked. "I mean, baby Superman could've been in there, and now he'd Russian, thanks to you."

Cross chuckled. "That's why I keep you around, Sergeant. I value your pragmatic, grounded sense of perspective."

Although he'd expected a return laugh out of Brighton, the Combat Controller's expression clouded over. "Now that you mention it," he said, "there's something I need to talk to you about." He paused for a moment. "Dyer offered me a job."

Cross wasn't surprised. Dyer's interest in Brighton had been obvious from the start. "With Phantom Cell, I take it?" Cross asked.

"Yeah," Brighton said, staring at his boots. "Apparently part of the reason they sent him out with us was to evaluate how I operate in the field. Did you know about this?"

"First I've heard of it," Cross said. A half-smile tugged at the side of his mouth. "You didn't really have to do much this time out, though, did you?"

"I saved Dyer's life," Brighton said. "As it turns out, that goes a long way in a job interview."

Cross grew serious. "Are you going to take his offer?"

"I don't know, man," Brighton said. "Should I? I'm qualified. I can do the work — probably better than anybody I know. It's a different kind of work, though. What do you think?"

Cross considered his response carefully. "I think Phantom Cell operates very differently than we do. Remember what Dyer kept obsessing about? The drone, the drone, the drone. He didn't care about the civilians. He certainly didn't care about the Russians. I'm sure he would've just as soon let us storm this place and kill as many 'bad guys' as we could in order to get that drone away from them. But it's like I told him before: that's not how we operate. If Phantom Cell *does* operate that way… is that something you want to be a part of?"

"They might not all be like that," Brighton said without much conviction. "But even if they are, I'm not. Maybe I can change things for the better."

"If anyone could, it'd be you," Cross agreed. "In any case, I can't make this decision for you, and it's not one you should be in any hurry to make for yourself. Give yourself time to think through all the possibilities. Just make sure you do what's best for you."

"All right, Commander," Brighton said, frowning in thought. "I'll let you know what I decide to do."

As Brighton walked away, Cross put his back to Lost Aspen and looked up at the sky. The phantom

sun's light shone dull and weak, casting a gloomy pall over everything. The South Pole's summer was almost over, and the cold winds hinted at a long winter still to come.

A shiver went up his spine — one that had nothing to do with the Antarctic cold.

2012.101
LOADING...

CLASSIFIED

MISSION DEBRIEFING

OPERATION

PHANTOM SUN 5678

PRIMARY OBJECTIVE

x Locate & secure crashed aircraft

- Maintain anonymity

SECONDARY OBJECTIVES

- Avoid hostilities with Russian forces

STATUS

2/3 COMPLETE

3245.98

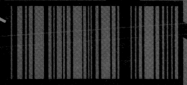

CROSS, RYAN

RANK: Lt. Commander
BRANCH: Navy Seal
PSYCH PROFILE: Team leader of Shadow Squadron. Control oriented and loyal, Cross insisted on hand-picking each member of his squad.

Our primary objective was to secure the crashed aircraft, but I refuse to believe that any piece of technology is worth risking forty-plus American lives, let alone waging war with Russian Special Forces. To my mind, we came away from this mission losing nothing except, possibly, a Combat Controller.

I have to admit that the thought of losing Brighton is unnerving. It would be hard -- maybe impossible -- to find a better man for the job...

Lieutenant Commander Ryan Cross

ERROR

UNAUTHORIZED

USER MUST HAVE LEVEL 12 CLEARANCE OR HIGHER IN ORDER TO GAIN ACCESS TO FURTHER MISSION INFORMATION.

2019.681

SHADOW SQUADRON

WHITE NEEDLE

WRITTEN BY
CARL BOWEN

ILLUSTRATED BY
WILSON TORTOSA
AND
BENNY FUENTES

2012.241

AUTHORIZING

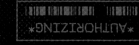

SCHOLASTIC INC.

CONTENTS

1316.981

ACCESS GRANTED

2012.101

CLASSIFIED

SHADOW SQUADRON DOSSIER

CROSS, RYAN

RANK: Lieutenant Commander
BRANCH: Navy Seal
PSYCH PROFILE: Cross is the team leader of Shadow Squadron. Control oriented and loyal, Cross insisted on hand-picking each member of his squad.

WALKER, ALONSO

RANK: Chief Petty Officer
BRANCH: Navy Seal
PSYCH PROFILE: Walker is Shadow Squadron's second-in-command. His combat experience, skepticism, and distrustful nature make him a good counter-balance to Cross's leadership.

YAMASHITA, KIMIYO

RANK: Lieutenant
BRANCH: Army Ranger
PSYCH PROFILE: The team's sniper is an expert marksman and a true stoic. It seems his emotions are as steady as his trigger finger.

BRIGHTON, EDGAR

RANK: Staff Sergeant
BRANCH: Air Force Combat Controller
PSYCH PROFILE: The team's technician and close-quarters-combat specialist is popular with his squadmates but often agitates his commanding officers.

PHOTO NOT AVAILABLE

JANNATI, ARAM

RANK: Second Lieutenant
BRANCH: Army Ranger
PSYCH PROFILE: Jannati serves as the team's linguist. His sharp eyes serve him well as a spotter, and he's usually paired with Yamashita on overwatch.

PHOTO NOT AVAILABLE

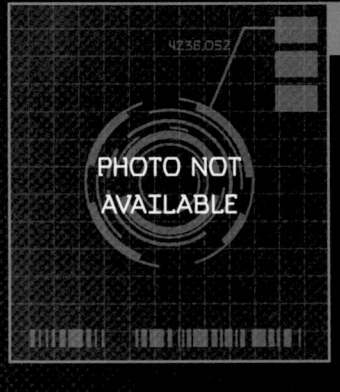

SHEPHERD, MARK

RANK: Lieutenant
BRANCH: Army (Green Beret)
PSYCH PROFILE: The heavy-weapons expert of the group, Shepherd's love of combat borders on unhealthy.

2019.681

CLASSIFIED

OPERATION

WHITE NEEDLE

5678

Syrian rebels have acquired a White Needle, or stolen chemical weapon. We already know they plan to use it, so it's our job to determine the target and prevent the launch. Two Israeli intelligence agents are willing to provide intel on the missing weapon in exchange for extraction from Syria. I'll be leading a team to rendezvous with them.

If we fail, gentlemen, it's likely that thousands of lives will be lost. I know we have the talent and technology to prevent that from happening. Let's get to it.

– Lieutenant Commander Ryan Cross

3245.98

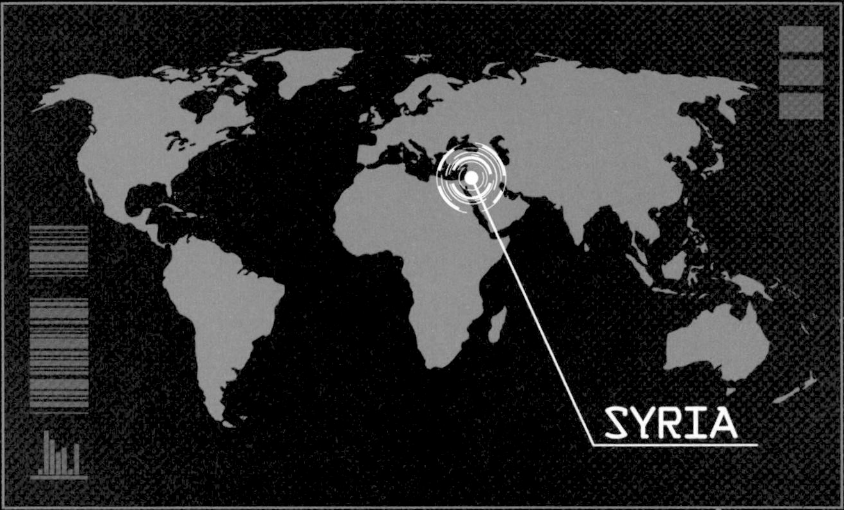

PRIMARY OBJECTIVE(S)

- Rendezvous with Israeli forces
- Recover missing chemical weapon

SECONDARY OBJECTIVE(S)

- Capture Syrian rebels responsible
- Limit enemy casualties

1932.789

0412.981

1624.054

5514.108

INTEL

DECRYPTING

12345

COM CHATTER

- CANALPHONE: an inside-the-ear two-way radio
- OVERWATCH: a small unit that provides tactics and intel from a good vantage point
- RECONNAISSANCE: the act of gathering intelligence
- UAV: UNMANNED AERIAL VEHICLE used to covertly gather intel

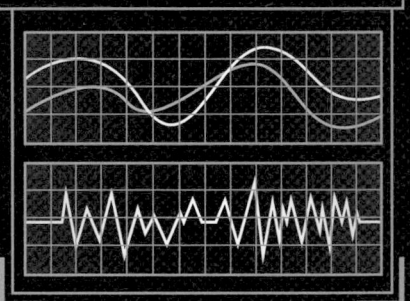

3245.98

CHAPTER ONE 1324.014

FRIENDLIES

Lieutenant Commander Ryan Cross led his four-man fireteam through the city of Al-Haffah, Syria. The center of the town lay ghostly and deserted. In the pale moonlight, the city's half-destroyed buildings loomed overhead like twisted fingers of dead giants trying to claw their way out from the earth.

"Lots of sniper holes, Commander," Lieutenant Kimiyo Yamashita informed Cross.

Yamashita was an experienced Army Ranger and the team's sniper, so Cross was inclined to take his word. Cross nodded. He directed the men to follow him closer to the cover of a ruined building nearby.

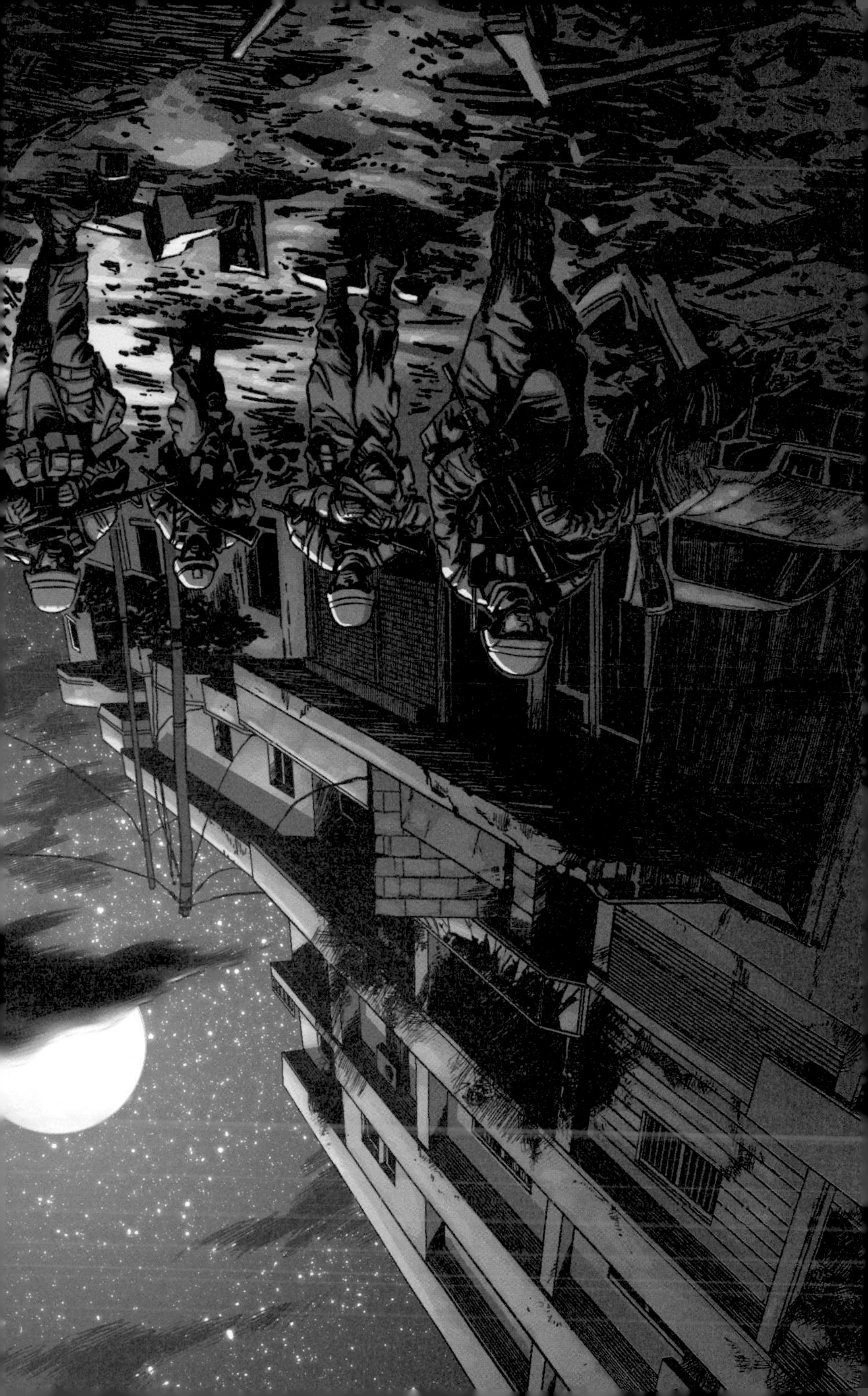

The town had been shelled by the Syrian army's artillery at the command of President Bashar al-Assad. He hoped to eradicate a group of rebels of the Free Syrian Army who had taken refuge there.

It was true that the overpowered rebels had fled to Turkey after the attacks, but Al-Haffah's battered landscape hardly looked like victory. To Lieutenant Commander Cross, the ruins suggested that Syria's president cared more about crushing the rebellion than he did protecting his people and their way of life.

The rebels of the Free Syrian Army would probably agree with Cross's opinion. In late 2010, much of Syria's citizenry had organized and carried out civil protests regarding the abuse of power by their government. The Syrian government responded violently to the protests, resulting in a civil war. While the United States, the United Nations, and other foreign entities would generally prefer to avoid interfering in civil conflict, President Assad's crackdown on rebels had been so brutal that the world couldn't stand by and do nothing.

The United States formally acknowledged the

rebels' Free Syrian Army (or FSA) as the true voice of the Syrian people. Nations on every border of Syria took in refugees who fled from the violence. A few allowed FSA rebels to hide on their soil while they regrouped and readied for the next battle.

For its part, the US considered itself invested in Syria's future. It had every reason to hope that the FSA would topple President Assad's ruthless regime. Hopefully, the Syrian government that arose from a rebel victory would take better care of its people's needs through a western democracy.

Aside from publicly voicing its support, the US government had taken no action to aid the rebels against their government. No weapons were donated, and no troops were deployed. To most of the world, America had taken no steps whatsoever.

Officially.

Unofficially, however, America involved itself in the Syrian conflict in one major way: It deployed Ryan Cross's Shadow Squadron.

Cross signaled toward a bombed-out house not far from the objective. "Take position there and get

ready to give us some cover," Cross said to Yamashita, his voice barely a whisper. "In case we need it."

"Sir," Yamashita said.

The top-secret unit was comprised of elite soldiers from all branches of the military. It attracted only the best of the nation's soldiers and employed them on ultra-sensitive, top-secret missions — even missions they couldn't officially (or legally) be involved in. Therefore, while the US government claimed to have no official presence in Syria, it did have its best men on site to keep an eye on things.

The main US concern was that Syria's government possessed vast stockpiles of chemical weapons. The Syrian government had even begun moving them within the country as if they were preparing to use them.

If the government collapsed and if the rebels weren't able to restore order quickly enough, there was a real concern that some of the chemical warheads would fall into the wrong hands. Terrorists, criminals — any madman among them could cause destruction and chaos with those weapons.

Complicating things even further, certain terrorist organizations had taken an interest in helping the FSA against President Assad's government. Al-Nusra Front, or the Front for Victory of the People of Syria, had been committing reckless bombings and paramilitary attacks against the Syrian army since the beginning of 2012. Most of the FSA disapproved of their extreme tactics.

The idea of helping such criminals and terrorists was distasteful to the US, to say the least. However, the possibility that these same criminals and terrorists might gain access to Syria's chemical weapons arsenal in the event of a rebel victory was far worse. That was the real reason Cross's Shadow Squadron had been mobilized to Syria.

Based out of the neighboring and allied country of Jordan, the eight-man team conducted special reconnaissance and direct-action raids against locations in rebel-controlled Syria. Their goal was to limit Al-Nusra's extremist influence on the Syrian revolution. To that end, Shadow Squadron had been coordinating with special operators from Israel to monitor the location of Syria's chemical

weapons. While they didn't work side-by-side with Israeli soldiers, they regularly traded information on persons of interest or chemical-weaponry parts.

One of these trades of information led Cross's fireteam to Al-Haffah early this morning. An agent of the Mossad — Israel's Intelligence Division — had arranged a trade of information that Cross was assigned to retrieve. Cross was used to being kept in the dark while infiltrating deep inside unfriendly territory, but he wasn't especially thrilled about it.

Cross turned to Second Lieutenant Aram Jannati, another Army Ranger. "I want you with Yamashita on overwatch," he said, handing over a tablet computer he'd been carrying.

"Sir," Jannati said, accepting the tactical pad from Cross.

With a tap on the screen, Jannati brought up a black-and-white image transmitted from the unmanned aerial vehicle (or UAV) hovering silently overhead. It had been following them ever since the fireteam set out. The UAV's low-light mini-camera provided a crisp, colorless image of the surrounding

area. It showed no obvious sign of civilians or nearby hostiles.

Jannati turned the tablet screen toward Yamashita. "Where do you want to set up?" he asked.

"Here," Yamashita said after thinking for a moment. He tapped the image of a half-destroyed roof on a two-story house. It sat on a hill a block from their destination. Jannati nodded.

"Go," Cross said. He tapped the two-way canalphone nestled in his left ear. "High Road, this is Low Road. We need you to reposition Four-Eyes for us."

"Roger, this is Low Road," Staff Sergeant Edgar Brighton's voice replied in Cross's ear over the comm channel. Brighton was a technical genius and a Combat Controller from the US Air Force. He had designed the small quad-copter UAV, and now he piloted it remotely from where the rest of Shadow Squadron waited. "Just tell me where you want it."

Cross relayed new coordinates as Yamashita and Jannati relocated to their overwatch position. That left Cross alone with Hospital Corpsman Second Class

Kyle Williams, the team's medic. "Are we expecting to need cover out there, sir?" Williams asked.

"You know what I know," Cross said. "There shouldn't be anybody out there except for our contacts and maybe a few scavengers. Still, better to have cover and not need it than to need it and not have it."

"Fair enough," Williams said. "But what's so important we need to go pick it up in person?"

Cross shook his head. "Command wouldn't say. Either the Israelis didn't tell them or it's above our pay grade."

Williams tried to hide a frown, but Cross saw it. He felt the same way Williams did. In his experience, dealing with the Mossad was pretty much like dealing with the CIA. Both organizations tended to give out only as much information as it took to get soldiers like Cross and his men in trouble.

"In position," Jannati informed Cross a few moments later.

"Four-Eyes is ready too," Brighton reported.

"Route's clear to the objective," Jannati added. "We'll let you know if that changes."

Cross acknowledged the reports with a quick double-tap on his canalphone. Then he nodded to Williams, and the two-man team set out.

They crept slowly through the shadows cast by the twisted bones of the ruined neighborhood. They kept their M4 carbines at the ready, but they saw no signs of life except for a scrawny dog sniffing among some overturned trash cans.

KRAKA-BOOM!

BA-DOOM!

From far and near came the rumble of exploding bombs and the crackle of distant gunfire. Sneaking through the eerie ghost town, Cross realized how glad he was that his own country hadn't descended into modern-day civil war. It was the stuff of nightmares.

The rendezvous point was a house at the end of a cul-de-sac. It had escaped direct shelling and gunfire but had still been seriously damaged. At some point,

a bomb had exploded near a car parked in the street, hurling the smashed vehicle into the front of the house like a knife. The wrecked car jutted upside-down from the wall by the front door.

"The back is clear," Jannati informed them over the canalphone.

Cross double-tapped his acknowledgement and led Williams around the back. No lights were on inside and no sounds came from within. Motioning Williams to take a position beside the rear door, Cross paused at the threshold. He gave three quick knocks.

NOK! NOK! NOK!

A moment later, a voice spoke from inside. "Jingle bells."

Cross gave a little smirk. "Batman smells," he answered, giving the agreed-upon password. Williams rolled his eyes.

"Wait," the inside voice said.

Cross heard a rattling of a makeshift barricade from inside. Then the door opened. A young Israeli

in black fatigues held a sawed-off shotgun pointed at gut level. He looked Cross and Williams over with obvious confusion, noticing the lack of any identifying marks on their uniforms. "You're the Americans. Are you CIA?"

"Nope," Cross said. "Do you have some intel for us?"

"Inside," the Israeli said, backing off and lowering his shotgun. He disappeared into the house, prompting Cross and Williams to follow him. Williams closed the door behind them.

"I'm glad you made it," the Israeli soldier said. "Which one of you is the medic?"

"I am," Williams answered before Cross could stop him.

"Our orders didn't mention anything about a medic," Cross said. It was sheer chance that he'd picked Williams to accompany him to the house.

The Israeli sighed. "So this isn't a rescue?" he asked. He paused at the threshold of an interior room. "I should've known."

"What's your name? Are you hurt?" Williams asked. "Do you need a medic?"

"My name is Benjamin," the man said, "and I'm fine. It's Asher who's injured. He's been shot." He headed into a nearby room.

Williams pushed past Cross and hurried into the next room with the Israeli. On a cot lay a second Israeli, who'd been stripped to the waist and heavily bandaged around his stomach with cut-up bedsheets. Williams knelt at the man's bedside and slung off his pack. The first Israeli leaned against the wall and looked down at his wounded comrade with tired worry.

"Hey, Asher, can you hear me?" Williams asked. He lay one palm over the wounded man's forehead and took his pulse at the wrist with his other hand. The man lay immobile and unconscious. Sweat gleamed on his skin, and a dark bruise peeked above the topmost edge of the bandage. "He's burning up." He looked up at the first Israeli. "Where was he hit, Benjamin?"

"In his back," Benjamin said. "On the right."

"Commander, please give me a hand," Williams said.

Cross knelt beside Williams. Together they levered Asher onto his left side. At Williams' nod, Cross cut away the bandage until only a thick square of gauze remained over the wound site. Deep, purple-red bruises covered most of the wounded man's lower back.

"Hold that there," Williams said. "No exit wound. Severe bruising. Non-responsive. How long ago did this happen?"

Benjamin took a moment to realize Williams was speaking to him. "Huh? Oh, yesterday. What time is it?" He checked his watch. "Maybe 24 hours ago. A little longer."

Williams winced. "That's not good," he said. He dug through his medical pack and produced a set of fresh bandages.

"What happened?" Cross asked.

"Stupid, blind carelessness," Benjamin said. "We were in the mountains in Salma, monitoring a rebel

cell. They were celebrating a victory and we were backing off to exfiltrate. We didn't realize they'd called up reinforcements to replace losses they'd taken. We blundered right into them, and they cut my team down. Asher and I got out and played *machboim* with them for a while until we found this place. They didn't seem too eager to follow us in here."

"Machboim?" Cross said.

"Hide and seek," Benjamin explained. "Anyway, when we got here I cleaned the wound and patched him up. I didn't think it was that bad at first. He just had a little bruising around the hole and very little bleeding. I thought we could wait for a rescue, but he's been getting worse all day."

"That's because he's bleeding internally," Williams said. He pressed stiff fingers hard into Asher's abdomen on the right side. The bruised flesh barely gave in at all. "See how rigid that is? His whole abdominal cavity is filling up with blood. He's got a high fever, which means he's got a severe infection. His pulse is weak and he's barely breathing. He's not

reacting when I poke him like this. It should hurt like crazy, but he's not even twitching."

"Can you take the bullet out?" Benjamin asked, trying to stay calm. "Will that help?"

"Judging from where it went in," Williams said, "it's probably at least nicked his liver, his spleen, or his kidney. For all I know it's sitting inside one of those organs like a cork. It's a miracle he's lasted as long as he has."

"Is there anything you can do?" Benjamin asked. "Anything at all?"

Williams put on his most calm, blank, professional expression. Cross had seen it once before in the field — the day Second Lieutenant Neil Larssen had been killed in action during a covert op on an oil platform in the Gulf of Mexico.

"I'm sorry," Williams said. "It would've been unlikely even if you could've gotten him straight to a hospital."

Benjamin's face darkened. "His sisters will be devastated."

Cross backed off to give the Israeli a moment to feel his grief. He quietly tapped his canalphone. "High Road, this is Low Road," Cross said. "We need a pickup for two friendlies, one injured."

"Injured?" Brighton's voice replied in Cross's ear. "Who's —"

"Not one of ours," Cross said. "We're taking them back to base."

Cross double-tapped his canalphone to clear the channel. "Overwatch," he said, "reel in and get ready for pickup."

"Sir," Yamashita and Jannati replied.

Benjamin stood. "Where will you take us?" he asked Cross.

"Home," Cross said, "with a brief stopover at our base. We'll do everything we can for your man, I promise you that. But you'll owe us some information for the extraction."

"I'll tell you whatever you want to know," Benjamin said. He watched Williams finish re-bandaging his comrade's wounds.

When Williams was finished, Benjamin crouched in the medic's place. He placed his hand on Asher's chest and hung his head. Quietly and calmly, he murmured an Arabic prayer for the dead and dying over his comrade's body.

Cross walked over to Williams and stood beside him. "He's not going to make it?" Cross asked, barely above a whisper.

The medic shook his head. "He's lost too much blood, Commander," Williams said. "They're not going to be able to do anything for him back at base that I can't just do here."

"Such as?" Cross asked.

Williams let out a small sigh. "Load him up on morphine to ease his suffering," he said.

Cross grunted. "All right. Our ride back to base is going to be here in a few minutes. Get Asher ready to move, and ease his suffering as much as you can." He lowered his voice. "But save the morphine. We're not home safe yet, and one of our men might still need it."

"Yessir," Williams said. "I just hope whatever intel these guys found was worth it."

"Me too," Cross said.

5514.108

INTEL

DECRYPTING

12345

COM CHATTER

- EMPLACEMENT: a site used for artillery or weapons
- INTEL: intelligence, or information relevant to a mission
- SARIN: a potentially lethal nerve gas often used as a weapon

3245.98

WHITE NEEDLE

Several hours later, Shadow Squadron had returned to its temporary base in Jordan.

Asher, the wounded Mossad agent, had died in transport. The Americans put his body on a plane back home to Israel. The other agent, Benjamin, agreed to an intensive interview with Cross and Cross's superiors via two-way satellite broadcast. The intel Benjamin's team had gathered filled the gaps in information collected by Cross's team. All the data went to a crack team of analysts back at Command.

That analysis painted a terrifying picture. Cross called in the rest of Shadow Squadron for a briefing.

The team convened in the mess hall stuck onto the meager barracks they'd borrowed from the Jordanian army. Cross set up a palm-size projector on the end of the mess table and synced it to the tactical tablet computer he cradled in one arm.

Cross quickly glanced across the room to make sure everyone was present. He tapped his tablet's screen. The projector displayed an image on the wall beside him. Chief Walker shut the door and took a position on the opposite side of the projection.

Normally Cross preferred Walker to sit with the men during a mission briefing, but this time he didn't mind the extra support up front.

"Well this can't be good news," Brighton whispered to Yamashita. "Walker and Cross aren't even glaring at each other."

Yamashita ignored him.

"We have a serious problem," Cross said. "An emergency interrupt just came down from Command. We're going mobile in one hour for a White Needle emergency."

Eyes widened on every face in the room. White Needle was code for a rogue chemical weapon and implied that it was in the hands of an enemy with intent to use it.

"Give them the background, Chief," Cross said, handing the tablet over to Walker. "The short version."

"Sir," Walker said, taking the tablet. He swiped away the first image to replace it with a dossier photo of an olive-skinned, bearded man in his late 50s. "You all remember our target, Abdul-mateen Shenwari. He's an Afghani mujahedeen who was behind bombings and raids in Afghanistan, Yemen, and Iraq. Intel confirms that he's up to more of the same stuff in Syria. He's organizing and helping supply cells of FSA fighters against President Assad's army."

Nods and low murmurs went around the room. Shadow Squadron had originally been tracking Shenwari in Iraq, but a rash of bad intel had allowed the criminal terrorist to slip through their fingers. When CIA informants declared that Shenwari had

resurfaced in Syria, Cross's team had been reassigned there to aid in ongoing operations. But Shenwari always remained one step ahead and just out of reach.

"The intel our Israeli friend provided helped us identify the top two locals working under Shenwari here in Syria," Walker said. He advanced the image on the tactical pad, breaking out two more dossier photos beneath Shenwari's photo. Both photos were taken secretly, as neither man seemed aware of the fact that he was being photographed. Both photos showed lean, hard-faced young Syrian men.

"The first one is Baltasar Dyab," Cross explained. "He's commanding a raid on an artillery emplacement overlooking the mountain town of Salma in the Latakia Governorate."

Walker nodded, then tapped the tactical pad. A map of the northwestern coast of Syria appeared. The towns of Salma and Latakia were highlighted on the map.

"The Syrian Army's been raining shells and missiles on the city of Salma for months," Walker

said. "So the rebels taking control of the emplacement is a pretty important local victory."

Walker advanced the image on the screen once more. A picture of Shenwari's other local lieutenant appeared. "Our Israeli friend was also able to confirm something we'd suspected but hadn't been able to prove," Walker said. "Last week, FSA rebels ambushed a supply convoy en route from Latakia. We knew that Shenwari's other top local man was behind the raid, but we didn't know much more than that. Now we do. The convoy was en route from a chemical munitions facility in the city, moving sarin gas to a secondary location. We thought the convoy and all its materiel had been destroyed, but Mossad's information indicates that the FSA actually made off with a large amount of sarin gas. Enough for a single warhead."

"How long have they known about this?" Yamashita asked with a scowl. "Surely not since before the raid."

"We believe they did," Cross said grimly.

"They knew this last week? And they're only just

telling us now?" Brighton asked. "What the heck were they waiting for?"

"They might not have told us anything at all if we hadn't extracted their men from Al-Haffah," Jannati said.

"That wasn't a favor," Yamashita said. "They knew their men needed extraction. They just *called* it an 'information drop.'"

"Didn't they think we'd help if they just asked?" Brighton asked. "I don't know if that's devious or lazy or —"

"But where's the connection?" Staff Sergeant Paxton asked, cutting in. "Between the convoy ambush and Salma, I mean."

Cross took the tactical pad back from Walker. He gave Paxton a grateful nod for getting things back on track. "All available evidence suggests that Shenwari has ordered his two lieutenants to regroup their separate forces in Salma with the sarin gas," Cross said. "Hence our White Needle emergency. Our own intel indicates that they are planning to arm and launch a chemical warhead from the artillery

position the FSA just captured. And signs point to sooner rather than later, before Assad's army can take back control of that emplacement."

"What's the range of their warhead from that position?" Paxton asked.

Cross swiped across his tactical pad and brought up a map of western Syria. The towns of Salma and Latakia were surrounded by a progression of rings that expanded out into the neighboring cities, as well as into Turkey to the north. Centers of high population density within those rings were all marked on the map, as well as important Syrian Army military bases and Turkish refugee camps to the North.

"As you can see," Cross said, "their range of attack is alarmingly large."

"How do we know they're planning to use what they have?" Sergeant Shepherd asked. "I don't see how it would benefit them. The western world is already on their side. Everybody's worried President Assad is going to use these things on his own civilians. What could the rebels gain from using the warhead?"

"It's Shenwari we're worried about," Cross said. "He's radical and unstable and dedicated to his jihadi cause. If he's got a weapon like this, he will use it — it's just a matter of time. Fortunately, our intelligence is ahead of the curve for once, and we've got a chance to stop him."

Cross placed his hands on his desk and leaned forward. "So we're heading to Salma to neutralize Shenwari's chemical weapon capacity," he said. "If we can recover the weapon or weapons, great. If not, we're authorized to destroy them. As a secondary objective, we're to kill or capture Shenwari if he's at the site. If not, we're to scoop up one or both of his lieutenants for questioning."

"Sounds simple enough," Yamashita said. "Are we coordinating with the Israelis on this?"

Cross and Walker both shook their heads. Cross kept his expression blank, but Walker's face betrayed some of the frustration both men felt.

"The Israelis are staying out of this one," Cross said tightly. "They say they've already lost too many men putting the puzzle pieces together for us."

Cross swiped and tapped on his tablet screen to bring up low-light camera footage taken from a high vantage point. It showed recent imagery of the Syrian Army's artillery emplacement in the mountains near Salma. It wasn't much to see, but it did give a decent idea of the emplacement's layout and size.

"That's footage from the Avenger UAV," Brighton offered.

"Correct," Cross said with a nod, clearly impressed that Brighton could identify the UAV solely by its photos. "It was taken a week ago — before the raid. We're trying to get a UAV or a satellite over the area to provide fresher intel, but this is the best we can do at the moment."

Cross paused to produce a laser pointer from his hip pocket. He shined it on the southern portion of the map. "We'll be inserting via Wraith from this direction..."

INTEL

DECRYPTING

12345

COM CHATTER

- AVENGER: a UAV, or unmanned aerial vehicle, used remotely for reconnaissance
- FROG-7: Soviet missile launcher
- LZ: landing zone, or where a helicopter touches down
- WRAITH: stealth helicopter

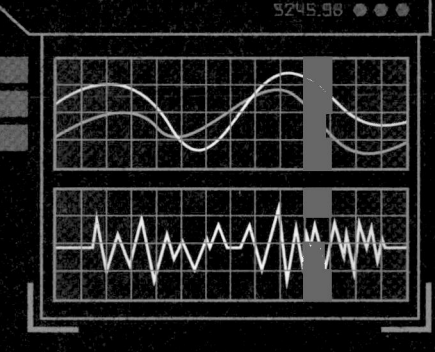

5245.98

CHAPTER THREE

1324.014

WRAITH

Within the hour, the team was in the air, aboard its Wraith stealth helicopter. A heavily modified Sikorsky Blackhawk, the Wraith used state-of-the-art scythe-shaped rotors, a radar-deflecting surface, and a host of other top-secret innovations. It was almost impossible to see in the night sky, detect on radar, or even hear unless it was right overhead. The muffled engine noise and reduced propeller turbulence made for an eerie stillness inside the passenger compartment, except for a strange humming sound. Cross had ridden in the Wraith plenty of times, but the unnerving hum still got under his skin.

"Go over the safety briefing again, Williams," Cross said. "Humor me."

"Sir," Williams half-said, half-sighed. He leaned forward on his bench seat. "The chemical in our White Needle is sarin. It's clear, odorless, and tasteless. You can be exposed through your skin, your eyes, or through respiration. It's heavier than air, so if it gets loose, it's going to roll right downhill."

"Right toward us," Brighton said. His insect-like, panoramic night-vision mask sat atop his head, leaving his expression clearly visible. Although he had a smile on his face, it looked sickly and strained.

"Yes," Williams said. "And it acts fast, so you're going to have to watch yourselves and each other for symptoms."

"And if you do notice symptoms," Cross added, "tell me immediately so we can get out of the area."

"Right," Williams said. "The signs to watch out for are: runny nose, watery eyes, drooling, sweating, headache, blurred vision, eye pain, cough, chest tightness, confusion, weakness, nausea..."

Cross nodded and let Williams trail off. What Williams didn't point out was that those symptoms indicated a relatively mild exposure to sarin. Higher concentrations of the deadly chemical would result in convulsions, paralysis, loss of consciousness, and respiratory failure — all within just a few seconds. There would be nothing Williams could do for them so it was best not to fill their heads with fear.

"Just out of curiosity, Commander," Brighton asked, "why aren't we doing this mission in full-on rubber chemical suits?"

None of Cross's men had voiced this question before now. Apparently, they trusted that their commanding officer had a compelling reason.

"For one thing," Cross said, "the odds of us coming in contact with actual sarin gas are minimal. The components Shenwari's locals stole are binary. They remain separate and harmless until the warhead mechanism mixes them into sarin in flight. If they do launch it via missile, we're not the ones who are going to have to worry about the gas."

Brighton and the others nodded. Apparently

the explanation set their minds at ease, even if it shouldn't have.

"Second," Cross continued, "this artillery emplacement is up in the coastal mountains, and we're going to be inserting downslope via Wraith to preserve the element of surprise. That means we're going to goat-foot it upslope, and take it from me — you do not want to do that in a full chemical suit. The lighter we travel, the faster we move, the sooner we get the job done."

"All right, Commander," Brighton said. "That makes sense." He paused for a moment then turned to Williams."But you're stocked up on whatever the antidote for sarin is, right?"

"I'm stocked up on atropine sulfate and diazepam," Williams said, patting his first-aid kit. Cross knew that wasn't exactly the cure that Williams made it out to be.

"He can also provide you one lollipop if you don't cry too much," Shepherd said, grinning, as he dug an elbow into Brighton's ribs.

Williams chuckled. "They're sugar-free," he said.

"Blech," Brighton said, sticking out his tongue. "I'd rather have the sarin."

"Quiet down," Cross said over the laughter. "We're just a couple minutes out from the LZ. Get squared away. It's almost time."

"Sir," the men murmured. Their faces turned hard and serious. Cross was glad for the break in the tension — he could always count on Staff Sergeant Brighton to provide one — but this was no longer time for jokes.

* * *

When the Wraith reached its destination, it paused high above the artillery emplacement occupied by FSA rebels, possibly commanded by Abdul-mateen Shenwari.

"Bird's eye is coming online now, Commander Cross," the helicopter pilot said through Cross's canalphone.

"Roger that," Cross said. "We're syncing up with you now."

Brighton made a few taps and swipes on the

tablet computer he held in his lap. A live feed from the helicopter's powerful fiber-optic cameras came on line. It wasn't as good as the feed would have been from Brighton's own Four-Eyes, but high winds over the mountains had forced them to leave his UAV behind. As the image became clear, Brighton looked up at Cross and gave him a thumb's up.

"We have a visual," Cross said. "Stand by to take us to the landing zone."

"Roger that," the helicopter pilot said. "Approaching the LZ."

"Huddle up," Cross said, half-joking. The interior compartment of the Wraith was hardly spacious when packed full of eight soldiers and their gear. Cross motioned for Brighton to hand him the tablet. He positioned it so all the men could see it.

Cross switched the overhead camera footage into a wide-angle view of the terrain. He overlaid it with contour lines showing the area's relative elevation. The overtaken Syrian artillery emplacement was little more than a flat, rocky ridge at the top of a gently sloping path. A flimsy wooden cabin had

been erected there at some point, likely to provide sleeping quarters for the artillery crew, but it had since been surrounded by tents. Three M116 75mm pack howitzers stood at the ready by the edge of the ridge. A flatbed truck that had likely transported the weapons was visible next to the tents. FSA rebels hung around the howitzers, but they didn't appear to be tending the weapons or preparing to operate them. There was no sign of ammunition for the weapons.

Between the howitzers and the nearby mortars was another truck. It was this one that drew Cross's attention: the boxy, eight-wheeled brick of a vehicle with a long, steel rail structure on top. A crane apparatus reached down over one side. Beside the truck, being lifted by the crane, was a 30-foot-long steel missile. The missile was a 9K52 Luna-M, more commonly referred to as a FROG-7. It had an effective range of 70 to 90 kilometers and could travel at a top speed of three times the speed of sound. In other words, the target would never hear it coming.

Most importantly, the FROG-7 was capable of launching a chemical warhead. And from what Cross could tell, the men clustering around the FROG-7

were preparing to deliver just such a warhead to some unsuspecting target. When the men in the Wraith realized this, they let out a collective gasp.

"Okay, then," Cross said. He tapped his canalphone to include the Wraith's pilot in what he had to say. "Guys, plan one is out. They're getting ready to launch down there, so we're escalating this to a full-court press. Our main objective is to disable that missile — and anybody who tries to get anywhere near it."

"I'm packing two Hellfire missiles, Commander," the Wraith pilot informed him. "I can blast that launcher apart from up here, if you like."

"The Hellfires don't burn hot enough," Cross said. "I can't risk a detonation throwing liquid sarin all down the mountainside and into the city of Salma."

"I suppose that's a fair point, Commander," the pilot said, his voice full of disappointment. "Negative on the Hellfires."

Cross smirked. "Actually, go ahead and put one into those howitzers," he said. "They should be far enough from the FROG-7 to minimize the danger."

"I can do that," the pilot said excitedly.

"After that I want a quick sweep with the miniguns across the open ground. Then get us down and let us out. Fast. You can hop back up here when we're clear."

"You got it," the pilot said.

"Guy sure seems to like his artillery," Brighton joked.

"I heard that," the pilot said.

"Chief Walker," Cross said, "I want you, Shepherd, Brighton, and Jannati out of the Wraith and down first. Yamashita and I will cover you, then you sweep us clear a space to follow you. When we're down, we'll make for the FROG-7 and eliminate the surrounding resistance. Once it's ours, Brighton will disarm and disengage the FROG-7's warhead. Then we hold position until the Wraith comes back and gets us outta there."

"Sounds simple enough," Chief Walker said sarcastically.

Cross didn't blame him. He knew that as soon

as he gave the order, all hell was going to break loose, and his simple, straightforward backup plan would be an exercise in barely constrained chaos. Fortunately, his men had surprise on their side.

"All right," Cross said. "Every man knows what he needs to do?"

The men of the Shadow Squadron nodded. "Roger that," the Wraith's pilot said through the canalphone.

Cross's heart rate sped up. The sour and cold taste of surging adrenaline made his lips peel back in a wild, involuntary grin.

"Let's do it," he said.

SS

5514.108

INTEL

DECRYPTING

12345

COM CHATTER

- HELLFIRE: air-to-surface missile
- HOWITZER: high-trajectory, high-power artillery
- M4 CARBINE: short and light automatic assault rifle
- TRACER ROUNDS: used in bullet magazines to track direction of gunfire

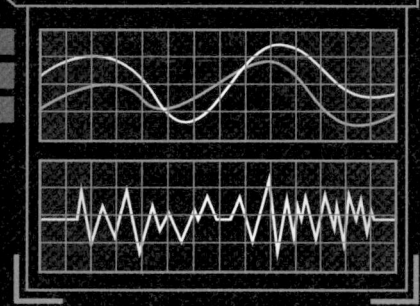

3245.98

CHAPTER FOUR

1324.014

FROG-7

The Wraith descended in a wide, spiraling arc, its nose pointed down toward the rocky ridge. Recessed panels on the Wraith's underside folded open, revealing two Hellfire missiles. At the pilot's click of a switch, one of the missiles lanced down into the cluster of unmanned pack howitzers.

KA-BOOOOM!

The howitzers exploded in a blaze of heat and thunder. Their twisted wreckage flew off the ridge and down the mountainside.

The pilot spun the Wraith in midair and launched the second (and last) Hellfire missile into the cluster of mortars on the other side of the emplacement.

WIRRRRRSH!

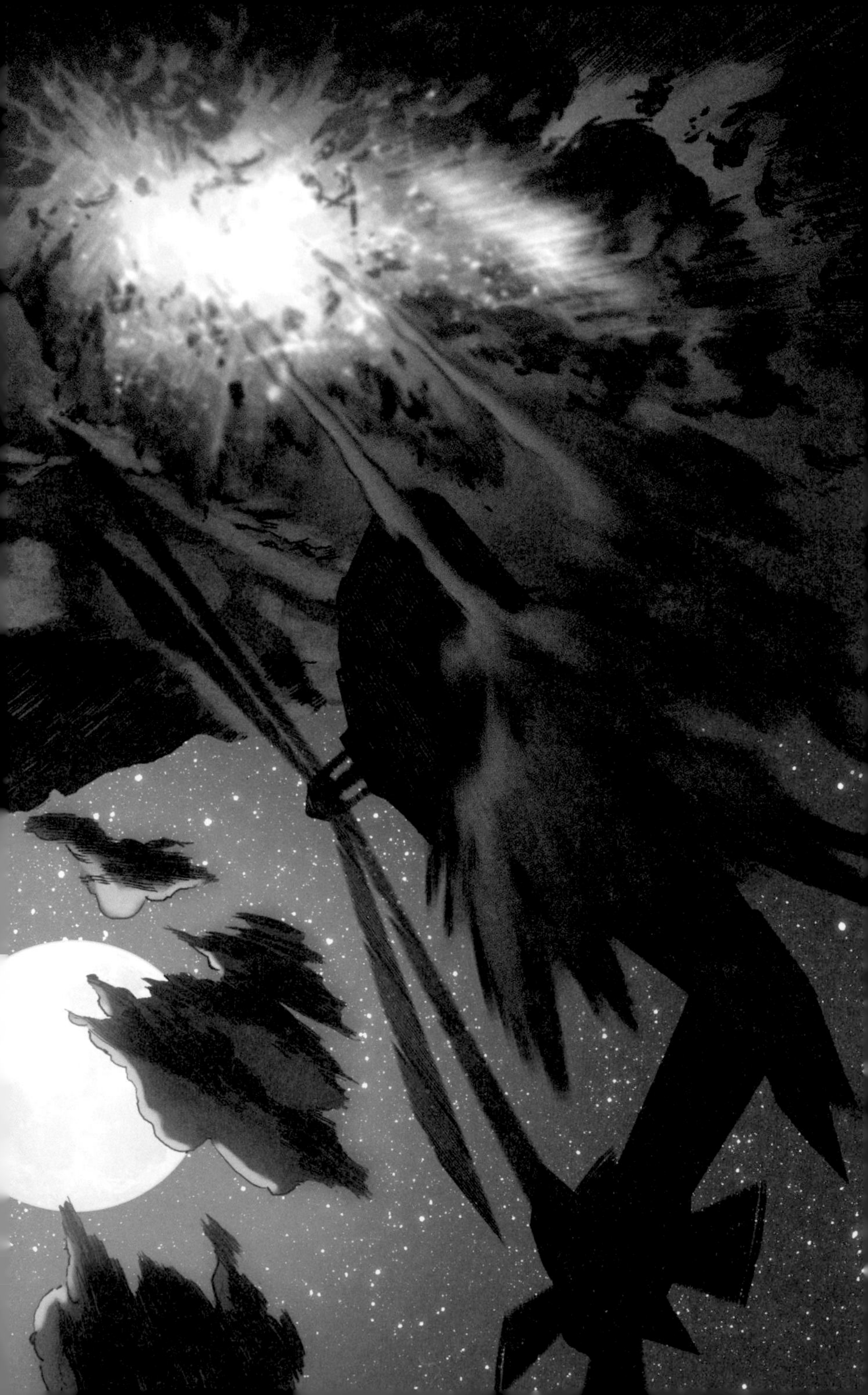

The smaller, lighter mortars disappeared in a cloud of billowing smoke and earth. There was no wreckage left behind. The vehicles parked near the mortars were damaged beyond repair, as well.

The pilot's assault couldn't have caused more confusion and activity. Rebels dashed out of their tents and out of the cabin and began running in all directions. With their weapons drawn, they tried and failed to find the source of the attack. To clarify the situation for them, the pilot made his presence more than obvious by opening fire with a pair of M-134 miniguns.

RAT-A-TAT-TAT!

RAT-A-TAT-TAT!

The miniguns laid down two tight streams of 7.62x51mm NATO rounds at a rate of nearly 50 rounds per second. The sun-bright lines of tracer rounds and the vicious power of the regular rounds scattered the soldiers, though not all of them were able to get to safety.

All the while, the Wraith descended toward the side of the emplacement that was farthest from the mountain road. When the chopper reached a safe height, it opened its doors and dropped a pair of rappelling ropes from each side. Walker, Shepherd, Brighton, and Jannati were already clipped onto the ropes to descend. Cross and Yamashita stepped forward and knelt in the opening next to the others.

"Go!" Cross ordered.

The first four-man fireteam stepped out of the Wraith and slid quickly down their ropes. Cross and Yamashita provided covering fire with their M4 carbines, picking off those few fighters below who had stood their ground and fired up at the helicopter. The two best shots in Shadow Squadron, Cross and Yamashita easily kept their fellow soldiers safe all the way to the ground.

The four men below unclipped themselves from the lines and formed up to move toward the FROG-7 launcher.

"Ready up!" Cross ordered. Then he, Williams, Yamashita, and Paxton clipped onto the ropes and dropped out of the Wraith to join their comrades.

As Cross's group slid down, those already on the ground took a knee and laid down suppressing fire. Walker and Jannati fired in three-round bursts from their M4 carbines. Brighton let loose with more intimidating and less precise blasts from his AA-12 combat shotgun, chewing up the side of the cabin where some of the gunmen had taken cover.

The most effective cover fire came from Shepherd. He tucked his M240 machine gun under one arm like a madman and swept it in an arc across the area.

RAT-A-TAT-TAT!

RAT-A-TAT-TAT!

It was a terrible firing position for a belt-fed machine gun, but it was undeniably effective at backing off the enemy force.

"To the FROG-7!" Cross said as his second team touched down and unclipped from the rappelling lines. A high-speed winch slurped the lines back up into the Wraith, and the helicopter disappeared into the night sky.

Brighton pointed toward the wreckage where the mortars and the rebels' parking lot had been. "RPG!" he shouted. The team turned to see a man with a rocket-propelled grenade launcher aimed at the Wraith.

Cross and Yamashita both fired a round with their M4s. Their target jerked and fell, firing just as his legs went out from under him. A line of white smoke shot upward through the air, missing the Wraith by mere yards.

"Yikes!" the pilot yelped in Cross's canalphone. "Thanks, fellas!"

"All clear, Wraith," Cross and Yamashita replied. They glanced at each other and cracked a quick grin.

"Go!" Cross ordered.

As one, Shadow Squadron rushed across the emplacement, dodging fire from the few FSA fighters who'd taken cover.

Shepherd kept the shooters pinned down with machine gun fire as he and Paxton brought up the rear. Unfortunately, a group of FSA soldiers had taken cover by the FROG-7, which Cross didn't realize until his men were right up on it. Two men popped out from behind the heavy truck to open up with AK-47s.

BANG! BANG!

BANG! BANG!

Brighton managed to nail one of them with a thunderous blast from his AA-12, throwing the man back against one of the launcher's tires. The other squeezed his rifle's trigger, spraying automatic fire.

POP-POP-POP!

POP-POP-POP!

The rounds hit Walker, Jannati, and Williams before a three-round burst from Cross cut the second gunman down. Walker was hit in the lower leg. Jannati caught two bullets in his ballistic vest. The last shot punched through Williams' upper right arm, missing his chest by less than an inch. Walker and Williams both cursed roughly. Jannati would have done the same if the shots hadn't knocked the wind out of him.

Cross ordered his team to establish a defensive perimeter and to secure the FROG-7 and its loader. Shepherd and Paxton took a position behind a line of waist-high rocks. They set up the M240 machine gun and opened up with it. Yamashita knelt beside them and added his deadly single-shot cover fire to Shepherd's more manic automatic fire. As the FSA fighters' return fire turned erratic, Paxton popped up and hurled an M67 frag grenade into the wooden cabin.

BOOOOOOOM!

The explosion rattled the structure and blew out its last remaining window. He threw a second grenade into the nest of ruined vehicles where most of the FSA rebels had taken refuge.

BA-ROOOOM!

In the wake of the second detonation, the return fire ceased. Murmuring voices and the whimpers of the wounded could be heard in the darkness, but no one seemed too eager to engage Shadow Squadron anymore.

While Shepherd, Paxton, and Yamashita were doing their work, the other five members of the team had their hands full securing the FROG-7. The rebels had finished loading the missile onto its launcher before Shadow Squadron had touched ground, and a team of tenacious gunmen had holed up around the machine to defend it. Two of those fighters had surprised the squad and wounded Williams and

Walker. At least two more men remained alive on the opposite side of the launcher.

As Williams helped Walker hobble over to the launcher, Brighton rushed over to them and helped Williams break out his first-aid kit. Jannati, meanwhile, shook his head clear and gulped down a deep, ragged breath. He'd found himself taking a knee next to the body of the man Brighton had shot. The body belonged to Sargon Balhous — one of Abdul-mateen Shenwari's top local lieutenants.

When Jannati had his breathing under control, Cross motioned for him to get up and move with him. Cross then motioned for Brighton to stay with Williams to aid and cover the medic while he tended to the injuries. Brighton gave a quick nod and hefted his AA-12 at the ready.

Cross led Jannati to the corner of the launcher and paused at the edge to listen. He heard two voices conversing in Arabic in desperate, rushed whispers. Cross heard the click-clacking of a computer keyboard and was able to make out the words "coordinates" and the Arabic phrase "Allahu yaghefiru liy."

Cross signaled for Jannati to follow him, then he vaulted over the high bumper of the FROG-7 truck and sprang around the corner at a high angle. Jannati came around a second later at ground level. The two FSA fighters on that side of the truck were ready for some sort of attack, but Cross's unconventional tactic caught them off-guard.

BANG!

The quicker of the two FSA men fired where Cross's chest should have been. Instead the shot hit only the empty air between his knees.

BANG!

BANG!

Cross shot the soldier in the shoulder and Jannati emerged a second later to finish him off. The second man was crouched over a mobile data terminal that was plugged into the side of the FROG-7 truck. Cross's second shot missed him by inches.

The man—none other than Shenwari's other local lieutenant, Baltasar Dyab—mashed one last key on the data terminal.

CLICK!

He looked up at Cross and Jannati with an expression of hopelessness. Tears gleamed in his eyes as he spread his hands and backed away from the keyboard.

Jannati raised his rifle and growled, "What did you —"

KIRRRRRRSSSSH!

A moment later, the roar of the FROG-7's rocket answered Jannati's question. Heat, pressure, and an unbelievable roar obliterated the capacity for rational thought. Cross and Jannati could only watch helplessly as a 30-foot-long missile loaded with sarin gas roared upward into the night.

5514.108

INTEL

DECRYPTING

12345

COM CHATTER

- HUD: heads-up display, or the visual overlay on a computer screen
- PATRIOT MISSILE: the MIM-104 is a surface-to-air weapon
- STINGER MISSILE: a portable, surface-to-air weapon
- ZIP-CUFF: a lightweight version of handcuffs

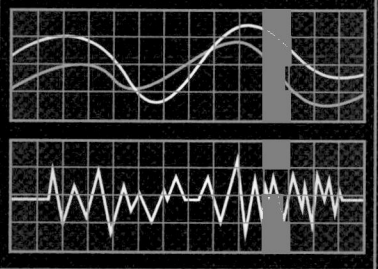

3245.98

CHAPTER FIVE

AVENGER

"Allahu yaghefiru liy," Dyab murmured. He was staring at the ground as the missile accelerated into the sky. He repeated the phrase over and over again.

Jannati raised his weapon to shoot the man down, but Cross raised a hand to stop him.

"Balhous is dead," Cross said. "We need this one alive if we're going to find Shenwari."

Jannati scowled. "Fine. I'll wrap him up." He ordered Dyab to lie down on his stomach and put his hands behind his back. The FSA fighter did so without complaining. He just kept muttering "Allahu

yaghefiru liy" over and over as Jannati bound his wrists with a zip-cuff from his pocket.

"Brighton, get over here!" Cross yelled.

Brighton had already come around the truck. He snapped his wraparound night-vision system up over his head. His eyes were saucer-wide.

"The rocket's up," Cross said, his voice flat but strained. "Can you—"

"Where's it headed?" Brighton asked. "I mean, Israel and Damascus are that way." He pointed south. "Turkey's that way." He pointed north. "And... well, nothing's west of here but the ocean."

"It's going into Saraqeb," Baltasar Dyab interrupted. "Allahu yaghefiru liy."

"Saraqeb's rebel-held, you idiot!" Jannati snapped, tightening the zip-cuffs on his prisoner's wrists.

"Can you stop it?" Cross asked Brighton. "Blow it up, turn it around, or something?"

"Not from here, man," Brighton said. "The FROG-7's not a guided missile. This launcher's not a remote

control. It's just a big truck with a rail on top. That's all."

"What can stop it?" Cross said. "The Wraith?"

"The Wraith won't be able to catch it," Brighton said. "Do we have any Patriot missiles nearby?"

Cross shook his head.

"Then I don't know," Brighton said, looking sick. "How about a miracle? Anybody owe you one of those?"

Cross grabbed Brighton by the shoulders and held him face to face. "People are going to die, Sergeant. They're counting on you. I'm counting on you. There must be something you can do!"

Brighton looked terrified. Cross forced himself to take a deep breath. He was only making things worse, and they were rapidly running out of time. If that warhead was heading for Saraqeb, they only had a few minutes to do something about it.

"Ed," Cross said slowly and calmly. "You can do this. If anybody can solve this problem, you can. So work it out. What do you need to get that missile out

of the air? Nothing's off the table. Just name it and I'll make it happen.."

Brighton closed his eyes and took a deep breath. He thought hard for what seemed an eternity of precious seconds. Then his eyes flew open. "Where's the Avenger?"

Cross felt a glimmer of hope. The Avenger was a modified General Atomics MQ-1 Predator Drone. It had high-quality cameras, a powerful engine, radar-deflecting stealth fuselage, and an array of air-to-air and air-to-surface missiles. Only the CIA and the Joint Special Operations Command knew it even existed.

"It's over Aleppo," Cross said, his excitement growing alongside Brighton's. "Is that close enough?" Aleppo, the largest city in Syria, was only 25 miles from Saraqeb.

"It'll be tight," Brighton said. "Get it moving toward us, then get me control of it. I'll bring that missile down."

"Command," Cross barked, opening the emergency channel over his canalphone. "I need a

hotlink feed from the Avenger's camera to my team's tactical pad and a secure line to Colonel Max Gordon in Colorado."

As Cross began sorting things out through channels, Brighton took the tactical pad out and plugged it into the truck's mobile data terminal. When he had them linked up, his fingers flew over the keyboard. Soon he had established a connection via satellite link to the US Air Force base back in Colorado where the top-secret Avenger unmanned aircraft was remotely piloted. He accepted the Command-approved feed from the Predator's cameras, but he hit a brick wall when he tried to access the drone's flight controls.

"I can't get in!" he cried. Hacking a top-secret Air Force command center with the equipment he had on hand wasn't realistic.

"Gordon, listen to me!" Cross was saying to the man on the other end of the comm channel. "I don't have time for this. This is a White Needle emergency and a Shadow-tier mission. Your people don't have security clearance for this. Just get us access to that UAV. Now!"

After a moment, Cross nodded. He looked at Brighton. "Okay, he needs to know our—"

"Just make him tell Lieutenant Wallace in their Security Department to stop fighting me," Brighton interrupted. "I can do the rest from here."

Cross relayed the information, then he moved to stand behind Brighton. The moment Colonel Gordon complied and allowed Brighton access to the Avenger's flight controls, Brighton stood up straight. He held the tactical pad out in front of him in both hands like a car steering wheel. The screen showed a front-facing camera view along with a complicated HUD that Cross could barely decipher.

"Got it!" Brighton said. "Interface is up, tablet's synced... And holy crap, I'm flying the Avenger!"

Cross marveled at what Brighton had been able to accomplish in less than a minute. By tilting and turning the tactical tablet, he was able to control the pitch, yaw, and roll of the Avenger UAV. Through an interface on the touchscreen, he also had control of acceleration and the weapons system. The interface was crude, but it was good enough for the problem

at hand. Brighton oriented the tablet, aiming the armed drone in the right direction. Then he opened the accelerator all the way up. Cross watched in amazement as the Avenger streaked westward from the Aleppo Governorate tearing across the sky toward Saraqeb.

"Won't take more than a minute, Commander," Brighton said.

"That's all the time we've got," Cross said. He stepped away from Brighton to check on the rest of his men. Jannati had led Dyab around to the other side of the launcher truck, where Williams was just finishing directing Walker in how to properly bandage the bullet wound in Williams' arm. A heavy bandage already shone white around Walker's calf.

"Report," Cross said.

"Area secure, sir," Walker said. It was ostensibly good news, but Walker's expression was clouded by a faint scowl. All along, Walker had made no secret of the fact that he wasn't happy having to potentially shoot and kill FSA rebels, even in the name of a greater good. "The rebels have all bugged out. The ones left alive, anyway."

"Good." Cross gave a whistle at the small covering fireteam of Yamashita, Shepherd, and Paxton. "Hey, guys, reel in. Get hands under these two and get ready for evacuation." He turned back to Walker. "Call the Wraith back in."

"Sir."

Cross came back around the truck to find Brighton staring hard at the tactical tablet. His fingers were white-knuckled from gripping too hard.

"All right, breathe, Sergeant," Cross said peeking over Brighton's shoulder. At some point, Brighton had switched the display to a thermal readout. The pinpoints of stars were gone from the night sky, and the city heat of Saraqeb glowed like plankton on the sea's surface. And in the center of the screen was a white-hot point of heat: the FROG-7 rocket.

"Is that it?" Cross asked. "Take it down."

"It's not close enough yet, Commander," Brighton said through clenched teeth. "Give me a second. Just give me a second..."

Cross watched the screen over Brighton's

shoulder, feeling just as tense as Brighton was. The rocket began to tilt downward, and Brighton tilted the tablet ever so slightly to cause the Avenger UAV to match it. Long, painful seconds went by, allowing the rocket to grow larger on the display. The lights of Saraqeb began to take up more and more of the screen.

"Brighton..." Cross urged.

"There!" Brighton shouted.

TAP!

Brighton jammed his thumb down on the weapons overlay on the UAV's heads-up display, launching the Avenger's full complement of air-to-air Stinger missiles. Glowing streaks of fire filled the screen. They rapidly closed in on the FROG-7 rocket. Brighton and Cross held their breaths as the missiles closed in on their target...

...and missed.

"What?" Brighton yelped. "No way!"

"Tell me you've got more of those," Cross said, fighting to keep the sudden fear out of his voice. "Sergeant?"

"Everything else is air-to-ground," Brighton said with a shrug. "I'd never hit that tiny little thing. But there's one thing left I can try."

"Whatever it is, do it," Cross said.

"I'm already on it, Commander," Brighton said. "Just one quick question: how much did the Avenger cost?"

Cross was about to unleash his rage at what seemed to be another of Brighton's smart-aleck remarks. Then Cross realized what Brighton was getting at as he watched him maneuver the Avenger down below the oncoming rocket.

Cross moaned. "Twelve to fifteen million dollars," he said, defeated. "Do it."

"My condolences to their budgeting department," Brighton said. He pitched sharply back and upward. When the FROG-7 reappeared on the Avenger's camera display, it took up almost the entire screen.

FZZZZZZZZZZT!

The feed from the Avenger disappeared. Brighton had crashed the UAV into the rocket, destroying both devices harmlessly high above the Saraqeb skyline.

Brighton lowered the tactical tablet and looked up at Cross. His shocked, adrenaline-flared expression was an exact match for the way Cross felt.

But when Brighton finally spoke, it was in a small, hushed voice. "I ain't paying for that, by the way."

"Me neither," Cross said just as quietly.

* * *

The Wraith carried Shadow Squadron and its prisoner back to the temporary base in Jordan. Dyab remained silent. Even when Cross told him that Brighton had destroyed the rocket and its entire chemical payload with no loss of life, the FSA lieutenant didn't even look up from his lap.

Cross glared down at Baltasar Dyab. "Why did you launch the rocket at Saraqeb?" he demanded.

Now the man did raise his eyes, but they were blank and hopeless.

"Answer him!" Jannati barked, shoving Dyab from behind with the sole of his boot. He clutched his chest where the bullet had hit his vest.

"Why Saraqeb?" Cross asked again, with a quick scowl at Jannati to calm the man down. "It's still under FSA control. Why target there?"

"Shenwari," the prisoner answered. "He convinced us it was a worthy sacrifice."

"Worthy?" Jannati snapped. "Thirty-thousand people live in Saraqeb! Rebels and innocent civilians…"

"Martyrs," Dyab said, his tone hollow. "He said they would be rewarded in Heaven and that Syria would be free."

Jannati was practically beside himself. Words failed him. Cross thought he understood what the Syrian meant, but he left it up to Walker to explain — which Walker had already taken the initiative to do.

"You weren't going to claim responsibility, right?" Walker said. "You were going to leave that position as soon as the rocket was away. That way, the entire world would think it was Assad's men who fired it on your people."

"Yes," Dyab said. "And then the rest of you, watching but never involving yourselves, then you would have to help us. That's what Shenwari said. Only he said you would reveal your true colors to the world by failing to help us. You would make excuses and —"

"Don't try to make this about us," Cross said. "It's not about us. It's not even about Shenwari, though he deserves some of the blame here. The fact of the matter is, the horror we stopped here tonight is all on you. You, Baltasar. You were the one who launched the rocket. You were the one who could've said no, but you didn't."

Dyab broke eye contact and hung his head. Whether he believed Cross or agreed with him, he gave no sign.

"Allahu yaghefiru liy," Dyab murmured,

retreating into his own internal world once more. "May God forgive me."

"We'll see," Cross told him. "We'll see."

CLASSIFIED

MISSION DEBRIEFING

OPERATION

WHITE NEEDLE

5678

PRIMARY OBJECTIVES

- Rendezvous with Israeli forces
- Recover missing chemical weapon

SECONDARY OBJECTIVES

- Capture Syrian rebels responsible

× Limit enemy casualties

STATUS

3/4 COMPLETE

3245.98

CROSS, RYAN

RANK: Lieutenant Commander
BRANCH: Navy Seal
PSYCH PROFILE: Team leader of Shadow Squadron. Control oriented and loyal, Cross insisted on hand-picking each member of his squad.

Talk about a close call -- and an expensive one. I'm just thankful that Brighton was able to save the day. These things really need to stop coming down to the wire, though -- my heart can't handle it.

I'm going to have to make this debriefing, well, brief since Command is on my case regarding operational expenses for this mission. Apparently "it was our only option" isn't a sufficient excuse for destroying a multi-million-dollar UAV. But I'll be sleeping well at night knowing how many lives we saved.

– Lieutenant Commander Ryan Cross

ERROR

UNAUTHORIZED

USER MUST HAVE LEVEL 12 CLEARANCE OR HIGHER IN ORDER TO GAIN ACCESS TO FURTHER MISSION INFORMATION.

2019.581

He's three years old, and I want him to read my books and feel the same way I did when I read my favorite books as a kid. And if he happens to grow up to become an elite soldier in the US military, that would be pretty awesome, too.

Q/Describe what it was like to write these books.

A/The only military experience I have is a year I spent in the Army ROTC. It gave me a great respect for the military and its soldiers, but I quickly realized I would have made a pretty awful soldier. I recently got to test out a friend's arsenal of firearms, including a combat shotgun, an AR-15 rifle, and a Barrett M82 sniper rifle. We got to blow apart an old fax machine.

Q/What is your favorite book, movie, and game?

A/My favorite book of all time is *Don Quixote*. It's crazy and it makes me laugh. My favorite movie is either *Casablanca* or *Double Indemnity*, old black-and-white movies made before I was born. My favorite game, hands down, is *Skyrim*, in which you play a heroic dragonslayer. But not even *Skyrim* can keep me from writing more *Shadow Squadron* stories, so you won't have to wait long to read more about Ryan Cross and his team. That's a promise.

CLASSIFIED

AUTHOR DEBRIEFING

ACCESS GRANTED

CARL BOWEN

Q/When and why did you decide to become a writer?

A/I've enjoyed writing ever since I was in elementary school. I wrote as much as I could, hoping to become the next Lloyd Alexander or Stephen King, but I didn't sell my first story until I was in college. It had been a long wait, but the day I saw my story in print was one of the best days of my life.

Q/What made you decide to write *Shadow Squadron*?

A/As a kid, my heroes were always brave knights or noble loners who fought because it was their duty, not for fame or glory. I think the special ops soldiers of the US military embody those ideals. Their jobs are difficult and often thankless, so I wanted to show how cool their jobs are and also express my gratitude for our brave warriors.

Q/What inspires you to write?

A/My biggest inspiration is my family. My wife's love and support lifts me up when this job seems too hard to keep going. My son is another big inspiration.

ARTIST

WILSON TORTOSA

Wilson "Wunan" Tortosa is a Filipino comic book artist best known for his works on *Tomb Raider* and the American relaunch of *Battle of The Planets* for Top Cow Productions. Wilson attended Philippine Cultural High School, then went on to the University of Santo Tomas where he graduated with a Bachelor's Degree in Fine Arts, majoring in Advertising.

ARTIST

BENNY FUENTES

Benny Fuentes lives in Villahermosa, Tabasco in Mexico, where the temperature is just as hot as the sauce. He studied graphic design in college, but now he works as a full-time illustrator in the comic book and graphic novel industry for companies like Marvel, DC Comics, and Top Cow Productions. He shares his home with two crazy cats, Chelo and Kitty, who act like they own the place.

2019.681

CLASSIFIED

CREATOR BIO(S)

AUTHOR

CARL BOWEN

Carl Bowen is a father, husband, and writer living in Lawrenceville, Georgia. He was born in Louisiana, lived briefly in England, and was raised in Georgia where he went to school. He has published a handful of novels, short stories, and comics. For Stone Arch Books, he has retold *20,000 Leagues Under the Sea*, *The Strange Case of Dr. Jekyll and Mr. Hyde*, *The Jungle Book*, *Aladdin and the Magic Lamp*, *Julius Caesar*, and *The Murders in the Rue Morgue*. He is the original author of *BMX Breakthrough* as well as the Shadow Squadron series.

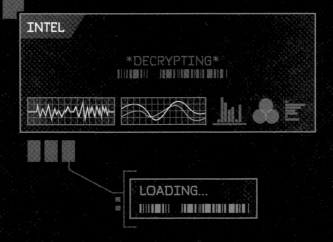

INTEL

DECRYPTING

LOADING...